Note to Readers

While the Harrington and Wakamutsu families are fictional, the events they face are real. During the last years of World War II, people of Japanese heritage were released from the internment camps and allowed to return to their homes on the West Coast. They often faced prejudice because people who had lost loved ones during the war with Japan took out their anger on their Japanese American neighbors.

At the same time, Americans were beginning to discover the horrible things that had been done to Jewish people and other minorities by the Germans. American and other Allied soldiers freed prisoners in concentration camps. They learned that millions of people had been tortured, starved to death, and killed in gas chambers in these camps.

Most people call World War II a just war because it was a battle against true evil. While we may not be involved in military battles, every day we can choose to fight against evil when we see bad things being done to others in our neighborhoods and schools.

COMING HOME

Veda Boyd Jones

PUBLISHING, INC.
Uhrichsville, Ohio

For my father, Raymond E. Boyd—
WWII veteran and my hero.

© MCMXCIX by Barbour Publishing, Inc

ISBN 1-57748-514-9

Published by Barbour Publishing, Inc , P.O. Box 719, Uhrichsville, Ohio 44683
http://www.barbourbooks.com

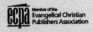

Member of the
Evangelical Christian
Publishers Association

Printed in the United States of America

Cover illustration by Peter Pagano
Inside illustrations by Adam Wallenta

CHAPTER 1
Eddie's Illness

Barbara Harrington tiptoed across the wooden floor to her brothers' room. If Eddie wasn't awake, she didn't want to disturb him, but Mama had sent her to check on him.

He'd had the sniffles for a couple of days, probably catching a summer cold, Barb had decided. He'd use about any excuse to get out of making beds and cleaning the hotel rooms. When she'd peeked in at lunch time, her twin had been asleep. Unless his headache had gotten a whole lot worse, she expected him to make a miraculous recovery and be up and playing now that the last bed had been changed and the final room swept.

Fully dressed, Eddie lay in the lower bunk bed with his eyes wide open, but he didn't sit up when she walked into the bedroom.

"Hey, Eddie, we finished the last room. You can get up now."

"I can't," he said in a terrified voice. "I've been trying to, but my legs don't work right." He lifted his head a little but didn't raise his shoulders off the bed.

"What do you mean?" Barb sat on the edge of the bunk. "You want me to pull you up?" She reached for his hands and was alarmed at how hot his skin felt. "You've got fever." That surprised her. She'd gotten it in her mind that he'd milked his summer cold for all that it was worth.

"Look," he said and lifted his arm as if it pained him and pointed to his legs. Barb could see his legs tremble through his pants legs.

The first thing she thought of was the absolute worst thing in the world. Polio. "Oh, no!" she exclaimed. Every summer Mama warned them to stay out of the heat of the day and away from the water. Wasn't that how kids got polio? But Barb hadn't heard of any cases this summer, and just a few days ago, she and Eddie had gone to the wharf to watch a troop ship leave Puget Sound. They'd stood in the afternoon heat right by the water, that deadly combination.

"Get Mama," Eddie said. His voice still sounded terrified.

Barb bolted out of the room, nearly tripping over the cat. A sense of urgency propelled her through the living room and out the apartment door to the lobby. Mama was sitting at the desk in the office, talking on the telephone. Barb ran to the office window.

"Come quick!" she said breathlessly.

Mama held up one finger and continued talking.

"Eddie's real sick," Barb gasped.

Mama looked up. "Excuse me," she said into the receiver. "Barb, is he vomiting?"

"He can't move his legs."

Mama dropped the phone, then picked it up again. "Emergency!" she said toward the receiver and didn't even say good-bye before slamming it down. She dashed out the office door and ran down the hall. Barb followed right behind her.

"Eddie!" Mama slowed down when she got inside the apartment and walked quickly to the boys' room. "Eddie!"

She leaned down on the bed and touched his face with the back of her hand. "You're burning up. Can you squeeze my hand?"

Tremors shook his arms. Barb watched the muscle spasms and saw her mother's face turn white.

"Mama?" Eddie said. "What's happening to me?" Panic colored his voice.

"Get Aunt Daisy's car and find Frank," Mama said. Barb raced to the hallway again, pounded on Aunt Daisy's door, and then ran to the back door. Frank had been in the alley behind the hotel after lunch, and he was still there, talking to some other high school boys.

"Frank! Come quick! Something bad is wrong with Eddie." Barb didn't wait for her brother. She left the screen door standing open and ran back down the hall. Aunt Daisy stood in the doorway of her apartment.

"Eddie's real sick. He can't move his legs," Barb said. "Mama needs your car."

Aunt Daisy wasn't really Barb's aunt, but she'd been living in one of the apartments for some time now, and the Harringtons had grown to love her. Her car was actually her son's car. He'd left it with her when he went to war.

Aunt Daisy grabbed her car keys off the key hook by the door.

"How long has he been sick?" she asked as they scurried down the hall.

"A couple of days, but not throw-up sick. I thought he was just ducking his chores."

The back screen door slammed shut and heavy footsteps thundered down the hall. Barb held the apartment door open for Aunt Daisy and waited a moment for Frank.

Mama stepped into the living room. Her face was still unnaturally white, and she held onto the couch. "Barb, call the doctor and tell him we're on the way to the hospital," she said in a hushed voice. "The number's in the office. Daisy, can you drive us? Frank, you'll have to carry Eddie. He can't walk."

A sob choked her voice. "He was all right this morning. Said he had a headache. He didn't mention his legs hurting. How could this happen so fast?" Mama shook her head, gained control, and held up her hand as Aunt Daisy moved toward her. "I'm all right. Let's take care of Eddie. Barb, can you manage the office? Can you handle that? The girls will be back some-time soon."

Barb sprang into action and raced to the lobby. The office door was still standing open. She went inside the small room and located the doctor's number on the important numbers sheet that Mama kept beside the telephone.

In a trembling voice, Barb told the nurse about Eddie. She was just hanging up the phone when Aunt Daisy flew by the office, her car keys held out in front of her as if doing that would cut a few seconds off her task of bringing the car around. She hadn't been out the front door but a moment when Mama and Frank walked around the corner of the hallway.

Between them, they carried Eddie. He was wrapped in a blanket, even though the July sun had raised the temperature to at least eighty degrees. Barb focused on his eyes, which were enormous. They were wide not with pain so much as with bewilderment. What was happening to him? Barb felt his emotions within her. That's what twins did. Sometimes she knew what he was going to say before he said it. And she most always knew how he'd react to things.

Barb stepped out of the office. She stared at him, and he stared at her, and an invisible cord stretched between them.

"You'll be all right," she said in an unnaturally loud voice. "I know you will."

He didn't nod, which was their usual signal to each other. Maybe he couldn't nod. Maybe the fever had drained him of his strength.

The little group made their way toward the top of the stairs. Outside, a horn honked. Barb glanced down to the street and made sure it was Aunt Daisy's car. She raced down the stairs, held the front door open, and then darted ahead of them to the car and opened the passenger door. Mama slid into the front seat and held Eddie on her lap. He looked odd half-sitting, half-lying on her. He was nearly eleven and almost as tall as Mama. Frank shut the door and hurried around to the driver's side. Aunt Daisy scrunched up and pulled the back of her seat forward so Frank could slide into the back. The door slammed, and they were off.

Barb watched until they disappeared out of sight. Then she turned and climbed the stairs to the second floor lobby. She took her place in the office. There really wasn't much to do, which was good. Her breath still came in gasps from all that running, and her heart was heavy with worry. "Dear God, don't let it be poli—" She couldn't say the dreaded word aloud for fear that it would make it real. "Please let him be all right."

She should call Dad, or was Mama doing that? They rarely called the Boeing airplane plant, and Barb didn't want to be the one to tell Dad anyway. What about her sisters?

Alice was at the clinic rolling bandages to send to the war. Isabel was at work at the Boeing plant. She could call Audrey, who had gone over to a friend's house after they'd finished the hotel work. Barb looked for the number, but she couldn't find it and discarded that idea.

Okay, she was here, and she could handle this. It wasn't the actual sitting behind the desk that bothered her. Fear for Eddie clutched at her mind and at her heart. She glanced at the clock on the desk and turned on the radio, which was usually kept on for the war news. Mama must have turned it off earlier when she'd answered the telephone. Bing Crosby was singing "I'll Be Seeing You."

The downstairs door opened, and footsteps ascended the stairs. They had a full house, and no one was checking out today, so if it was a stranger, all she had to do was tell the person that there was no room available.

"You in charge today, young lady?" the mailman asked.

"For a while," Barb said.

He handed her a bundle of letters, then turned and made his way down the stairs.

Barb had never sorted mail before, but she could do it. She knew she could. The boxes were numbers, and most of them had names on them. With the housing shortage in Seattle, the Harringtons had more permanent renters than those who came in for only a few days. Apartment boxes were on the top row, then the hotel rooms. That was one of the improvements that Dad had installed once they had taken over the hotel while the owners, the Wakamutsus, were in the Japanese relocation camp. Dad liked organizing things. That's what made him so good as an engineer. He liked details.

The little clock on the desk ticktocked, but there was no news from the hospital. Barb half-expected her mother to call. Or maybe there was no time. Maybe. . . No, she wouldn't think the worst. Think positive. Think positive. She prayed for Eddie's recovery. She begged God to make him be all right.

Barb poked thin letters into the boxes and had to force herself to keep working once she discovered a letter from Steve in the pile. She quickly finished putting up the mail and then pulled scissors from the desk drawer. With the sharp edge, she unsealed the letter. The paper was so thin, she didn't dare risk tearing it, for Steve would have written over every inch.

Her oldest brother was a pretty good war correspondent. This time the letter was whole. There were no cutout sentences. He hadn't written anything the censors would cut out with their razor sharp instruments. Barb had seen censors at work on the newsreel at the movies. Troop movements were too important to have leaked in case letters fell into enemy hands. The letters the family got from Steve were written weeks, even months earlier. Sometimes they would receive more than one letter a day. Sometimes they wouldn't get anything from him for several weeks.

She searched the top of the letter and found what she was looking for—June 16. He had written the letter after the D-Day invasion! The family had been waiting and waiting for news. After Barb had seen newsreel footage of the Normandy assault, she had understood the danger soldiers had faced. But if Steve had been part of D-Day, he'd made it through alive and well!

She celebrated that news in her heart and listened to the clock on the desk ticktock, ticktock.

"Mail come?"

11

Mr. Wiley stood at the office window, and Barb was glad she could hand him a letter. His grandson had been headed for England when he left, but now Mr. Wiley figured he was in Italy or France.

Mr. Wiley lovingly fingered the thin letter. "So Tommy wrote his old grandpa." He gave a pleased smile and shuffled back to his room. The next time she saw him, he'd tell her everything Tommy had written. He always did.

Barb read and reread Steve's letter. He was doing fine but was looking forward to a home-cooked meal when the war was over. He was tired of the rations the army gave him. And he was tired of walking in mud.

Where was Steve? Barb wondered. She wanted her brother home again and safe. She glanced at the clock. Not quite an hour had passed since Eddie had been taken away. What was the doctor doing to him now? She wanted Eddie home and safe, too. And she wanted to be back in their own home, in the big room she shared with Audrey. When the war was over, they'd get to move back home and out of the hotel. The Japanese owners would take it over, and then her life would return to what it had been like before the war started. Except she really didn't remember much about her day-to-day routine before the war had taken over their lives and they'd moved to the hotel more than two years ago.

Eddie had never liked the hotel chores. She wished she hadn't accused him of trying to get out of cleaning the rooms.

Mr. Denton wheeled down the hall in his wheelchair and collected his mail, and he started a small stampede down the halls. Once the mail came in, word traveled fast through the building. Mama had once commented on how glad she was when she could hand mail over to the residents instead of telling them there was nothing for them.

"You'll probably get news tomorrow," Barb told disappointed residents. She imagined Mama had told them that before. And she knew how they felt. She wanted news of Eddie right now.

Why didn't Mama call? Would the doctors have put Eddie in an iron lung? No, that was the worst. Surely he could breathe on his own. She would think the best. For the hundredth time since Eddie was carried to the car, she sent a prayer heavenward.

The clock on the desk ticktocked, ticktocked.

A man with an old plaid suitcase climbed the stairs and asked for a room, and Barb suggested another hotel down the street. She listened to a special radio program on the V-1 flying bombs that Germany had launched on England. No roar of planes overhead had warned the people that bombs were coming. The first bomb had made a buzzing sound and then exploded, flattening two hundred homes at one time.

Would the Japanese launch the V-1 bomb on Seattle? Fear tightened its grip on Barb's heart. She took deep breaths and watched the minute hand slowly move on the face of the clock.

Another hour passed. Finally she heard Audrey's voice drift up the stairs. Alice was with her, and it was clear from their footsteps that they were slowly making their way up to the lobby.

Barb wanted to shout at them to hurry, but why? There was nothing they could do but wait for news. She watched the stairs until their heads appeared. They didn't resemble each other at all. Alice was blond like Mama, and Audrey had curly dark hair like Dad's and Barb's. And Eddie's.

Barb had remained calm while time had crawled by all afternoon. But now with her sisters there to give her support, she felt a great sob rise up from her heart to her throat.

"Eddie!" The name was barely recognizable as she said it through tears.

"Barb! Where's Mama?"

"What's wrong?"

Both girls spoke at once, and Barb's tears rolled down her cheeks. When she could talk, she told them Eddie's symptoms.

Alice gasped. "Poli—"

"Don't say it!" Barb interrupted. "It can't be. We were only at the wharf the day the troops went out, and he didn't play in the water." That was what Mama constantly warned them about. "Stay out of the afternoon sun, and don't get in the water." Barb knew that warning by heart. But Eddie couldn't have the dreaded disease because even though the day had been warm, the sky had been overcast that afternoon. It had rained before they got back to the hotel.

The girls took turns standing at the window, sitting on the desk, and sitting in the lone chair behind the desk. They stared at the phone while the clock ticktocked.

When Barb didn't think she could stand it anymore, the downstairs door opened, and she heard familiar voices.

The girls rushed out of the office to the stairs. Below were Aunt Daisy, Mama, and Frank. No Eddie.

They didn't say a word until they reached the lobby.

Her voice full of weariness edged with fear, Mama said, "It's polio."

CHAPTER 2
Barb's New Job

"No!" Barb cried and flung herself into Mama's arms.

"It's not as bad as it could be," Mama said. She patted Barb's back and rested her cheek on Barb's head. "The tremors are just in his legs now."

"Is he in an iron lung?" Barb looked up at her mother, hoping against hope that Eddie wasn't having a machine breathe for him.

"No, honey. His lungs are still okay, but he's in a special ward."

"Can we see him?" Audrey asked.

"Only through a glass divider. Girls, we have work to do. We must burn his bedding and scrub anything he's touched in the last two days. Barb, can you take care of the desk for a while longer? Did you get the mail sorted?"

Barb drew away from Mama's arms. "It's all put up." She went back into the office as Mama and the girls, followed by Frank and Aunt Daisy, walked down the hall, dividing up the chores of disinfecting the apartment.

What about the rest of the hotel? Was everyone exposed to polio? Maybe everyone would move out. Then what? They were running the building for their friends, the Wakamutsus. Barb really didn't know them well. She'd been very young when her family had come to Seattle and lived in the building for a couple of years before they'd moved to their very own house. But Dad and Mama valued the Wakamutsus' friendship. What would the Japanese family say if they returned from the camp where they had to live during the war and found the place empty?

That was the least of Barb's worries. And there was nothing she could do about it, so she dismissed it and concentrated on Eddie. She had asked God to not let him have polio. But God hadn't answered that prayer. Eddie had the dreaded disease. Would it do any good to pray that Eddie wouldn't be paralyzed? She didn't know, but she'd been taught to pray, so she did. She prayed as hard as she could that Eddie would be home soon, running and jumping, playing baseball, and trying to outdo her, just as he'd always done.

In an effort to take her mind off her troubles, she concentrated on the words and sang along with songs on the radio, and she handed out more mail as some of the residents returned from their jobs.

When Isabel, dressed in coveralls, came in from her shift at the Boeing plant, Barb didn't tell her about Eddie. She'd let Mama do that. When Dad came home, she again maintained her silence about her twin. When he'd asked what she was doing in the office, she'd told him to go see Mama. She couldn't talk about it yet. She was too stunned by the terrifying news to do

16

anything but block it out of her mind as best she could.

She gave out a couple more letters. Aunt Daisy didn't have any mail from her son. And there sure wasn't any news for Alice from her fiancé. Jim Watson had been missing in action for more than two years. Alice hadn't given up hope that he'd return safely, but secretly Barb had.

"Barb." Dad stood in the doorway of the office. The fear in his eyes mirrored hers, and in two steps he had enveloped her in a huge hug. Once again Barb sobbed. When her tears had subsided, Dad handed her his handkerchief. "How much mail is left?" he asked.

She glanced at the neat boxes. Only a few still held letters. "Four," she said.

"Let's deliver them, and then we'll close the office. We're going to the hospital to see Eddie."

"Me, too?"

"Especially you," he said.

Together they walked the halls and slipped the letters under the residents' doors. A few minutes later, the family loaded into Dad's car, and he drove them to the hospital.

"You can just see him through a window," Mama explained. "He's going to be all right. We have to believe that."

Barb wanted desperately to believe Mama. But could she? Aunt Daisy had said she must think positively about things. Think that Steve would return safely from the war. Think that the United States would win the war. Think that life would return to normal. Now she could add to her list think that Eddie would be okay.

At the hospital, the family huddled in the hallway to look through the large window, about six feet long and three feet wide. Barb stood on tiptoes and peered through the glass. She spotted Eddie on the third bed. He lay on his back and stared at the ceiling.

"What are they putting on him?" she asked. Two nurses scurried from bed to bed and were now at Eddie's side.

"Hot, wet towels," Mama answered. "They're to help with the tremors, and we hope they will prevent paralysis."

Eddie must have felt their stares, for he turned his head slightly and looked right at them. His face clouded up, and Barb could see his tears even through her own tears.

"He needs us," Barb cried.

"Yes, he does," Mama said. "Wave at him and smile. We must be strong for him." Another nurse walked into the polio ward, and Mama knocked on the window to get her attention. "Don, there's the one we need to talk to." She turned to the others. "Would you all wait outside? Dad and I'll be out in a few minutes."

Frank held the exterior door for the girls, and they stood near the entry, waiting for their parents.

They talked about burning Eddie's sheets and clothes in the alley. One of the girls mentioned it was fortunate that he hadn't been in the hotel rooms the last two days. He hadn't contaminated them. At the time Barb had thought she was unfortunate, since she'd had to make up extra beds. Eddie had been painting walls and repairing screens in room nineteen with Frank and Ronnie Denton, the hired boy.

Mama and Dad joined them outside.

"What did you find out?" Alice asked.

"What did the nurse say?" Isabel asked.

"Let's get in the car," Dad said.

The group silently piled into the car and looked expectantly at Dad, who turned in the driver's seat to face them.

"His leg tremors are continuing. The head nurse thinks they will lessen soon, but we have to wait and see. The hospital is short-staffed right now, and your mom is going to stay at the hospital with Eddie. That means everyone must take on extra chores to fill in for her."

"When we get home," Mama said, "we'll make a list of chores and assign them. Since I won't be there to remind you, you'll check off the chores as they are completed."

"Are you coming back here tonight?" Barb asked.

"Yes. Eddie's scared."

Barb nodded. She had seen that in his eyes. If she were in Eddie's place, she'd be scared, too, and she'd want Mama right beside her. But would that be dangerous for Mama?

Dad started the car. Barb remained silent for the ride home but listened to the others talk about dividing up the chores and making sure the hotel ran smoothly.

Back inside their apartment, Mama made a list of all the things she did. Barb had no idea there were so many things. Everyone was on room detail, which meant sweeping floors and changing sheets as usual. Alice volunteered to take over the cooking, and Audrey said she'd be in charge of laundry. Barb was assigned to clean the hallways, lobby, and stairs every morning.

"I can put up the mail in the afternoon," Barb said.

Mama looked thoughtfully at her. "You did quite well today, even though you're young for the job. Alice could open in the mornings, and if you took the afternoon office shift, then the girls could continue with their volunteer work." She nodded. "Okay, that's a good plan. But if you find you can't handle the office, Barb, you must tell Alice or Audrey."

"I can do it," Barb said. And she felt confident that she could. She felt proud that she'd managed that afternoon, and she'd been under an enormous weight of worry then.

They divided up the other chores, with the older girls taking

19

the biggest load, although Frank took his share. Mama packed a bag, and Dad took her back to the hospital. When he returned he looked weary, and the others gathered around him for any new word about Eddie.

"The doctor won't be back until tomorrow, but whenever she can, Mama will call the office to report on his condition. Now we must pray for Eddie's and Steve's safety," Dad said.

"Oh, we have a letter from Steve," Barb said. "He wrote it after D-Day. I'll be right back." She took the key from the nail beside the door and ran to get the letter. How could she have forgotten such an important letter? It wasn't that Eddie was more important than Steve, but Eddie was here, and Steve was at an unknown place. She wished she knew where.

Once Barb made it back to the apartment, Dad read the letter aloud. "I think it would be best if we didn't tell Steve about Eddie," he said. "Steve has enough to worry about without adding another burden. When Eddie is home again, then I'll let Steve know what the family has been going through."

"But what should we say about Eddie? I always write Steve what we're doing. Won't he think it strange if I don't mention him?" Barb asked.

"Tell him that Eddie is playing chess with your mom. She took the chess board to occupy him. And another thing. . ." He looked at each one of them for a long moment. "I'll post a notice about Eddie's illness on the office door. If people ask, tell them that we've disinfected the area and that the hotel isn't under quarantine. We don't want a panic situation."

"We've only scrubbed our apartment," Alice said.

"But we're about to work on the lobby and the stairs—the public areas. Thank the Lord that Eddie's movements have been limited to room nineteen the last two days. Eddie is the youngest in the building, and polio usually strikes children, so our renters shouldn't worry unnecessarily. The danger of infection will be over shortly. But if you hear of anyone in the building being sick, we must alert them, in case they didn't see the notice."

Barb stared at her father. Without saying the words, he had told her that she was the most likely to get the disease. She felt her face. Was it hotter than normal? What were the signs? She wiggled her toes inside her shoes. They worked fine.

"Barb?"

She glanced at her dad and then at the others. Her sisters and brother had their heads bowed. She quickly bowed her own and added her fervent prayer that she, in addition to Eddie and Steve, would be safe.

Dad wrote the notice and tacked it on the door, while the girls got mops and buckets and strong disinfecting soap and started on the stairs and lobby. Frank tackled the back staircase and mopped out room nineteen. Barb and Dad scrubbed the walls and floor of the hallways. They worked until nearly midnight, but when they were finished, every surface was clean.

First thing in the morning, Barb repeated her prayer for safety and checked out her legs. They worked. She hoped Eddie's muscles had stopped trembling and were moving normally by now. With a heavy heart and the weariness of worry, Barb, along with Alice, Audrey, and Frank, moved quietly around the hotel, doing chores.

When time came for her afternoon shift in the office, Barb grabbed an armload of books from the low table in the living room and carried them to the office. She wanted plenty to do while she was cooped up in the small area.

The time went by pretty fast. Her best friend, Carolyn Weiler, came by, and Barb explained that Eddie was in the hospital and she was taking over the office so Mama could nurse him.

Carolyn cried when she learned Eddie had polio.

"But we think it's a mild case, and he'll be okay," Barb hastily assured her. "He has to be."

She actually felt closer to Carolyn than to her sisters, since they were older. Recently she and Carolyn had been in cahoots to torment Eddie and his friend Warren and to beat them in their war efforts in both scrap collections and Victory garden produce. But once they discovered that working together was better than competition, they had settled down some. Still, Barb believed a little friendly competition was always good.

Carolyn's brother had been killed at Pearl Harbor. She hated Japs with a vengeance, and so did Barb. How could she not hate someone who had killed Carolyn's brother? Mama told her that they should not hate, but they were at war. An enemy soldier could kill Steve. Barb hated Germans, too, since it was more likely that Steve was in Europe right now than in the Pacific. She wished she knew exactly where he was.

Carolyn promised to take over the twins' part of weeding their Victory garden and left for home. The mailman came, and Barb put the mail in the boxes and distributed it to residents who came to the office. There was no letter from Steve, so she reread the one that had come the day before and wrote a reply. The Wakamutsus had written. She didn't open that letter, but Audrey did when she came to the office to see how things were going.

"Yoshiko moved out of the camp," Audrey said, summing up the letter as she read. "She got a sponsor and a job in Chicago and was allowed to leave Idaho. The family misses her, but they're glad she's no longer behind the barbed wire, like they are. The boys have organized a baseball team. That's just like them," she said with a smile. "They love baseball as much as Frank and Eddie."

Barb was acquainted with the Wakamutsu boys—Kaneko, who was Frank's age, and Abiko, who was a year younger—but she didn't know them well. Oh, she'd been around them when their family had come to her house for Sunday dinners, but the older kids did things, so she and Eddie stuck together and played by themselves. Sometimes, the Harringtons had visited the Wakamutsus at the hotel. On those occasions, Barb and Eddie had walked around the streets and window shopped at the various businesses located on the edge of the international section.

Suddenly the phone rang. It was Mama reporting that Eddie's fever was lower. That was a good sign. She didn't mention how his legs worked, and Barb didn't ask.

"How are you feeling, honey? Are you tired?"

So her mother was worried that Barb would get the disease.

"I'm okay. I've put up the mail and most of it is out." Barb told her about the letter from Steve that had come the day before and the one from the Wakamutsus. "No one else is sick here," Barb told her. She had conscientiously asked everyone who came for mail how their family members were. So far, so good.

The days fell into a pattern. By week's end, Barb had settled into her new job. Carolyn came over in the afternoons and stayed an hour or so. She said she liked sitting in the small office, too, and might grow up to be a secretary. Mrs. Hunter, who lived in apartment six, came to the office precisely at four o'clock every day. That was when her favorite radio show ended. Every day she had a different complaint. Mama called about the same time each day to report about Eddie. The mailman maintained a fairly rigid schedule, too. No one in the building was ill, and Barb discovered each morning that all her toes and fingers worked. Maybe God was listening this time. Maybe He had been too busy listening to soldiers' prayers to hear her prayers about Eddie not having polio.

By the beginning of the second week, Barb was desperate for new activities to pass the long hours behind the desk. She missed Eddie. She missed arguing with him, playing with him, and going places with him.

"How's Eddie?" Carolyn asked when she came over. "Can he move his legs yet?"

"He's making progress," Barb reported. That's what Mama and Dad said. Just the night before the family had gone to the hospital to wave at him from behind the glass. This time he'd waved back, but one leg wasn't gaining strength like they had hoped. She didn't want to dwell on that and was glad when the radio program changed. "Oh, listen, it's news time."

As the correspondent talked, Barb wrote "France" in the margin of the newspaper. At supper she would relay the news she'd heard while in the office. Each night the family listened to Edward R. Murrow report the latest battles, but first they got Barb's report.

"I wonder if Steve's in France," Barb said.

"Why don't you ask him?" Carolyn suggested.

"He can't tell us. You know the censors would cut that out in a flash."

"Maybe he could give you hints."

Barb got Steve's latest letter out of the drawer. "He mentions mud, but that could be anywhere. Before D-Day, the censors missed his letter because he mentioned a town in England, and it wasn't cut out. We looked it up on the map, so we knew where he was." She opened the atlas that she'd carried down to the office and showed her friend the exact spot where Steve had written he'd gone to a movie when he'd had a rare night off.

Carolyn tapped her finger on the map. "Do the censors read your letters to Steve?"

"I don't know. I could ask him where he is, but what good would that do? He can't tell us."

"He can't tell you town names or country names, but what if you made up a code?"

"A code! Carolyn, you're a genius. I'm just mad I didn't think of that myself."

Barb pulled a sheet of paper out of the drawer. "I think our code needs a real piece of paper." Because of the paper shortage, they usually wrote on scrap paper, but this would be a code they could refer to every time they wrote to Steve.

She was hungry, so she thought of food words. "For 'France' we'll use 'pie.'" That was a treat they had not had since Eddie had gone into the hospital. Alice said she was no good on pies and had been saving the sugar so Mama could make a couple of them when Eddie came home.

"What about 'steak' instead of 'England?'" Carolyn suggested.

For the first time since Eddie had gotten sick, Barb felt excited and challenged. She eagerly set to work thinking of words for every country in Europe.

CHAPTER 3

Eddie's Homecoming

"How's Raymond doing?" Barb asked from the office window where she was working the afternoon shift.

Aunt Daisy looked up from the letter she'd just opened. "It's hard to tell." She held up her son's letter. All the holes reminded Barb of the snowflakes she'd cut out for the school bulletin board last winter.

"Raymond wasn't thinking about the censors when he wrote this one. I can't make out a whole sentence. Listen to this. 'We rode down to the blank where Cecil Woodall had left the truck. The tires were a foot deep in blank. We thought we'd need it for blank, but the lieutenant said we'd have to blank.' There are more blanks in this letter than words."

"You need the code," Barb said and opened the desk drawer.

She pulled out the code sheet that she and Carolyn had devised and handed it to Aunt Daisy.

"You think this will work?" Aunt Daisy asked after Barb had explained the system.

"I don't know. It's been three weeks since I sent it to Steve, and we haven't had a letter where he used it. He probably doesn't have my letter yet."

"I need to add code words. Raymond shipped out of Seattle. If he went to the European front, he would have sailed from back East, not from here. What can we use for Philippines or Hawaii or other island words?"

Barb opened the atlas to the Pacific Ocean, and she and Aunt Daisy made a new code. They used names of flowers for the various Pacific islands.

"We can't use 'daisy' for one of them, since that's your name," Barb said with a chuckle.

It felt good to laugh. There hadn't been much to laugh about lately. Eddie was through the worst of his illness, and although Mama came home at night, she stayed at the hospital with him during the day, helping him with exercises.

The hotel was running smoothly, but the family had to work more hours to keep everything going all right. People moved from one job to another, and Dad had complained that there had been quite a turnover of workers at Boeing since war production had begun. That also meant people moved in and people moved out of the hotel, and there were more rooms to clean thoroughly.

Aunt Daisy had helped a few mornings with the office so that Alice could work in the rooms alongside the others. When Eddie came home, Mama would go back to mornings in the office when most of the checkouts occurred, and Eddie would help again in the rooms. At least, Barb hoped he would. The latest report from the hospital had not been that good, although

Eddie was gaining strength day by day.

The phone rang. Barb handed the flower code sheet to Aunt Daisy and reached for the receiver.

Mama's voice held guarded excitement. "The doctor says Eddie can probably come home on Friday. He'll still have to do his exercises, but he'll be home."

This was Tuesday. Three more days. Barb's heart repeated the refrain. Three more days. Three more days. They could put up a big sign for Eddie, and maybe Alice could bake a cake. Carolyn could come over, and Eddie's friend Warren, too.

"I'll tell the others," Barb said. "How's his leg?" One had been responding to exercises, but the right one still wasn't doing well.

"He won't be walking when he comes home, but maybe soon," Mama said. "We must hope and pray for the best."

"Any mail for me?" Mrs. Hunter was at the office window, having nudged Aunt Daisy aside with her large bulk, and was demanding immediate action even though Barb was on the phone. Barb shook her head. "Well, do you have the newspaper?"

"I can hear Mrs. Hunter," Mama said. "Better take care of her. I'll see you this evening, Barb."

"Bye, Mama." Barb hung up and handed the afternoon newspaper to Mrs. Hunter, who never bought one of her own, but instead came down to borrow the Harrington's copy of the *Seattle Times* every afternoon. The first time she'd acted like she was going to take it back to her apartment, but Barb had told her she had to read it in the lobby in case someone else wanted to see it. She didn't know if that was Mama's policy, but Mrs. Hunter just grumbled and settled herself on the low couch, so Barb figured that Mama had told her that before.

Aunt Daisy moved to the window again. She was the exact

opposite of Mrs. Hunter. She looked on the positive side of everything, which she always told Barb was the sunny side and the only way to be happy. Mrs. Hunter could find wrong in everything and everybody. Those two women were night and day, breakfast and supper, sweet and sour. Barb grinned at Aunt Daisy and shook her head.

"Eddie will be home on Friday. Three days."

"We must plan a homecoming party," Aunt Daisy said. "How's his leg?"

In a sad, quiet voice, Barb recounted the little she knew.

"He shouldn't come home too soon," Mrs. Hunter said from the couch. "He could still spread the disease."

"No, he can't, or the doctor wouldn't send him home," Barb said.

"Are you being impertinent, Barbara Harrington?" Mrs. Hunter asked.

"No, ma'am. I'm just saying what I think. Eddie hasn't had fever for some time. Mama wouldn't bring him home if he could spread polio to the rest of us."

"I guess he won't be tearing around the place like he usually is."

Barb couldn't believe Mrs. Hunter would actually say that.

"No. He can't walk yet," Barb said coldly.

Mrs. Hunter had the grace to look flustered. "Oh, I didn't know."

"She couldn't have heard what you told me," Aunt Daisy said in a whisper. "She didn't know."

"He'll walk soon," Barb said. "I know he will."

The next day when Carolyn came for her afternoon visit, she and Barb planned Eddie's homecoming party.

"We need a big banner," Carolyn said. She waved her hand

in the air as if reading from a large invisible sign. "Welcome home, Eddie!"

"We don't have that much paper," Barb said.

"What else could we use to make it?" Carolyn asked.

Barb thought a moment. Frank and Audrey's high school had a banner made of cloth that the band carried in parades. Maybe she and Carolyn could use a sheet for the background, but Barb didn't know of any scrap material they could use for the letters. She glanced around the office. The last few days' newspapers were stacked in a corner waiting to be taken to the collection site.

"Oh, we can cut letters out from these newspapers and pin them onto a sheet," Barb said. "Then we can unpin them and use them for the paper drive."

Carolyn drew large letters on the newsprint, and Barb cut them out with the office scissors.

She paused to read a front-page story about the Americans capturing the island of Guam. She and Aunt Daisy hadn't made a code word for Guam. They'd need to. The article summed up the war in the Pacific and mentioned in passing the horrible Bataan Death March when the Americans in the Philippines had surrendered to the Japanese more than two years ago.

"I think Jim Watson is dead," Barb said. "Alice prays about him all the time, and she keeps saying he's coming back, but I don't think so." If he was captured, he'd have been forced to walk miles and miles, day after day with no food or water and then be put in a horrible prison camp. Barb didn't think he could last through that. "I hope he died in the fighting instead of having to go through all that torture and then die."

"He wasn't listed in the paper," Carolyn said and pointed to the daily column that listed names of the local men who'd been killed in the line of duty. She drew a big 'E' on that page.

"Mama said the Japanese didn't sign some agreement, so they won't give out the names. That's why he's listed as missing. The navy doesn't know where he is."

"The dirty Japs," Carolyn said through gritted teeth. Her eyes shone with tears. "I hope every one of them gets killed." She sniffed. "Mama is okay most of the time, but yesterday she was fixing supper and she just sat down on the kitchen floor and cried. She'd been cutting up a chicken, and I asked for the wishbone, and she said when Kenneth was my age, he always asked for the wishbone."

Barb didn't know what to do for her friend, whose tears were running down her cheeks. She patted her on the back. Barb hadn't known Carolyn's brother. He'd been killed before the Harringtons had moved back to the hotel and before Barb and Eddie had enrolled in Carolyn's school. Her friend didn't have any sisters, and now she didn't have a brother. Barb couldn't imagine what it would be like to have only her parents as a family.

"Do you have a handkerchief?" Carolyn asked.

Barb shook her head.

"I only have this one, but I can't use it." Carolyn pulled a lace-edged handkerchief from her pocket. Embroidered on one corner were a palm tree and the word *Hawaii*. No, she couldn't use the special one that Kenneth had sent her.

"Use this," Barb said and handed her a scrap of newspaper left over from when she'd cut out the letter *c*.

Carolyn wiped her cheeks and blew her nose on the newsprint, which left black ink across her face.

"Oh," Barb said. "You should see yourself." She grabbed the small mirror that hung on the wall and held it in front of Carolyn. "Your face is streaked with black."

Carolyn's mouth dropped open, and she squealed. "I look like someone painted me."

Barb thought Carolyn was going to start crying again, but instead she laughed. She hooted, and Barb felt laughter bubble up inside her. Soon the girls were laughing so hard, tears spilled from their eyes.

"Use this," Carolyn said and handed a newspaper to Barb. She wiped her cheeks and looked in the mirror. Her face matched Carolyn's.

"What's so funny?" Mrs. Hunter stood at the office window. "What have you two gotten into?"

"Nothing." Through gales of laughter Barb asked, "Would you watch the office while we go wash up?" Not waiting for an answer, she opened the office door and dashed for their apartment with Carolyn right behind her.

When the girls returned to the office, they were clean, and Barb carried a sheet and a pin cushion stuffed with straight pins. Mrs. Hunter was talking through the office window to a short man wearing a brown suit. On the floor beside him sat two suitcases.

"May I help you?" Barb asked and went inside the office. There was hardly room for her and the large woman beside her.

"He wants a room. Isn't thirty-two vacant?" Mrs. Hunter asked.

"Yes. How long will you be here?" Barb asked. She filled out a form just like Alice had shown her, had him sign it, and gave him a room key. The man picked up his suitcases and headed down the long hallway. "Thank you for watching the office, Mrs. Hunter."

"You're welcome," she said, but she made no move to leave the small room. "What are you making?" She waved to the newspaper letters on the desk and the pile on the floor where Carolyn had been drawing the letters.

Barb explained about the banner.

"You'd have more room if you worked out there on the floor," Mrs. Hunter said, pointing to the lobby. "Stretch that sheet out across the couch to pin the letters on." Without hesitating, she handed the scissors and pencil through the window to Carolyn. "Here." She thrust the letters and the unused newspapers at Barb.

Mrs. Hunter was one pushy woman, but this time she had a point. There was more room to work in the lobby. While Carolyn pinned letters on the sheet, Barb quickly cut out the remaining letters. By the time Carolyn had to leave for home, the banner was finished.

"Looks terrific," Carolyn said. "Where can we hang it?"

"In his bedroom, I guess," Barb said. "No, maybe in the living room. Mama says he has to do exercises, so he shouldn't be in bed too much." They folded the sheet, careful not to dislodge any pins.

"Tomorrow we'll plan the food," Carolyn said. "We need a cake. I'll see how much sugar we have at home. And I'll tell Warren."

As soon as Carolyn walked down the stairs and waved from the bottom step, Barb went back into the office.

"Thank you for watching the office, Mrs. Hunter. I'll take over now."

"Sure you don't have anything else you have to do?" Mrs. Hunter remained seated in the desk chair.

"No, this is my job for the afternoon."

The phone rang, and Mrs. Hunter grabbed the receiver. "It's your mother," she said and placed the receiver on the desk.

Barb looked pointedly at the woman, and with reluctant movements, Mrs. Hunter stood and walked out of the office.

"Thank you again," Barb called.

"Why was Mrs. Hunter in the office?" Mama asked.

33

Barb explained. "I was only gone a few minutes, but it was hard to get her out of here."

"She's a lonely woman," Mama said and then went on to tell Barb that Eddie was doing very well.

"Good," Barb said. "We're planning a surprise for him."

"Oh, he's planning a surprise for you, too."

No matter how Barb pleaded or cajoled, Mama wouldn't reveal the secret. Nor would she tell the family anything that evening when she came home.

The next afternoon, Carolyn and Barb worked on making more decorations. Since they didn't have balloons, they cut streamers out of more newspapers to tie in bows everywhere they could. Carolyn also announced that her mother had said they had enough sugar to make a cake.

Aunt Daisy said she'd also make a cake to celebrate Eddie's return so everyone could have a big piece. Everything was set for the next afternoon. As soon as Mama called the office to let them know that Eddie had been dismissed, Aunt Daisy would drive to the hospital and get them.

But the call came in the morning. Alice was running the office when Mama phoned. The doctor had come early and dismissed Eddie. As soon as Aunt Daisy could get there, he could come home. She left immediately for the hospital.

Daily work at the hotel came to a standstill. Barb called Carolyn, and she called Warren. They both hurried over to the hotel, Carolyn carrying a cake fresh from the oven. Frank, Audrey, and Barb hustled about, hanging the banner, tying streamers on every chair, curtain rod, and candlestick in the living room.

They finished the work and rushed to the lobby to await the honk of Aunt Daisy's car. The plan was for Frank to carry Eddie up the stairs, and then they'd all yell, "Welcome home, Eddie!"

"They should have been here by now," Audrey said after the welcoming group had paced the lobby for fifteen minutes and made countless trips up and down the stairs to the street below.

"Maybe they had a flat tire," Warren said.

"Are you waiting for me?" Eddie said from the hallway. Mama stood beside him, and Aunt Daisy stood behind both of them.

As one, the group turned toward his voice.

"Eddie, you can walk!" Barb exclaimed.

CHAPTER 4
Madam President?

Barb stared at Eddie, then rushed toward him.

"Careful." Mama stepped in front of him before Barb could reach him. "He can't walk very well yet, but he wanted to surprise you."

Aunt Daisy carried crutches and placed one under each of Eddie's shoulders. He looked less tense now that he had some support. Lines in his forehead smoothed out.

The others crowded around him.

"Are you in pain?" Carolyn asked.

"Can you go to school?" Warren asked.

"Did you walk all the way up here from the back steps?" Frank asked.

"One at a time," Mama said. "We don't want to overwhelm him."

"I'm okay, Mama," Eddie said with some of his old forcefulness. He turned and took a few awkward steps down the hall toward the apartment.

"Mama and Aunt Daisy carried me up the stairs to here. I'm not real good at walking yet, but I'm getting better." He touched the wooden crutch to his right pants leg, and Barb heard a clunking sound. "This brace under here helps keep my leg straight."

Barb's gaze shot to Carolyn's. They'd discussed the posters of polio kids with both legs in braces. Did a brace mean that Eddie would never regain use of that leg? Mama had said he was getting stronger. Didn't that mean that he would return to normal and be able to run and jump?

The group followed Eddie in a slow procession. Each of his steps seemed to take incredible concentration, and Barb found herself moving in the same way as Eddie with the same limp. She wasn't trying to mimic him, certainly not make fun of him. She was trying to help—trying to take some of the burden from him, but she knew there was no way she could.

Mama held the apartment door open, and as soon as they were all inside the apartment, Barb gave the signal. Immediately everyone yelled, "Welcome home, Eddie!"

"We have cakes to celebrate," Barb said.

"I could eat a couple of pieces," Eddie said. "Maybe three."

Mama laughed. "Eddie's been without sugar for a long time." She helped him sit on the couch with his legs stretched out.

Alice cut Eddie a big piece of cake, then she took a piece

with her and rushed back to the office. Audrey served the others, and they chatted with Eddie.

Barb wanted to cut all the chitchat and ask if Eddie would ever be able to walk without the brace. She knew he'd been having trouble with that one leg, but she'd thought that it would get stronger. Mama had mentioned time and again that Eddie was exercising it. Now it appeared that he had no control of it at all. Barb could see the ugly brace where his pants leg didn't cover it. She tried to look away, but her gaze kept coming back to his leg stretched out on the couch. Above his sock, the leg looked thin and bony. Tears stung her eyes, and she quickly got up and walked into her bedroom.

"Barb," Mama said from the doorway of the girls' room. "Are you all right?"

"I thought he wasn't going to be crippled," Barb said. Her voice caught on a sob. "I thought he was going to be all right. But he isn't, is he?"

Mama crossed the room and hugged Barb. "He is all right. He's not going to die from polio. That he has to wear a leg brace is a reminder of how much worse it could have been. We should thank God that Eddie's not in a wheelchair like Mr. Denton," she said. "Before long Eddie will be able to walk without crutches, and knowing him, he'll be running not long after that."

"With a limp."

"Yes, with a pronounced limp. But he'll be walking."

"I prayed that he'd be all right." Barb pushed away from Mama and plopped down on the bed.

"He is all right," Mama said once more.

"But I prayed that he would be back to normal. God didn't listen to me," Barb said defiantly and stood up. She couldn't sit still. She couldn't stand still. She wanted to strike out, to do something to release the anger she felt at Eddie being cheated by life. At the beginning of the summer, he'd had a whole body. Now he had one shriveled leg.

"Barb," Mama said, "God listened, and He answered your prayer but not with the answer you wanted. Good will come from Eddie being crippled."

"What?"

"I don't know, but when bad things happen to us, God sometimes uses the situation so that we can learn and grow as people. We must have faith." Mama handed a handkerchief to Barb. "Now dry your eyes and go be with Eddie and your friends. Eddie needs you to be strong. Accepting that he will be crippled hasn't been easy for him, either. He's still fighting it. He hasn't given up on a miracle restoring his leg."

Barb sniffed and wiped her tears. "Me, either."

With her head held high, she walked back into the living room and talked with the others about school starting in a couple weeks and about the ever-present war. She sat down on the floor beside the couch where Eddie lay. She needed to be near her twin after a month of being away from him.

"We've gathered tons of paper," Warren said and looked purposefully at the banner made of newspaper letters.

"We can use those," Eddie said, "but not for a little while. I like seeing my name like that."

Carolyn laughed. "The Girl Scouts are collecting paper, too."

Barb had been so busy with hotel work and running the office in the afternoon, that she hadn't had time to go out collecting. Instead, she'd made a place in the lobby for people to put their used paper.

"Oh," she said. "We didn't finish the rooms."

"How many do you lack?" Mama asked in the normal business tone she used for hotel matters. For an instant it seemed that things were back to normal. If only Eddie wasn't stretched out on the couch and could hop up and race Barb down the hall to finish their chores.

Reluctantly, Barb stood up. "We'll be back within the hour," she said.

Mama left Aunt Daisy, Warren, and Carolyn to occupy Eddie, and she went with Barb and the others to finish cleaning the empty rooms and making the beds.

"Will Eddie be able to go to school?" Barb asked when they had finished the last room and were headed back to the apartment.

"If you help him, I think he'll be okay," Mama said. "He's got to practice walking. We can't risk him falling down. That could further damage his leg."

That afternoon, Barb convinced Eddie that he could walk to the office and keep her company while she worked her shift. Mama didn't offer to take over, so Barb figured that job was still one she'd do until school started. She carried an extra chair to use in the office while Eddie sat in the big chair behind the desk.

"I sort the mail like this," Barb said after the mailman had left a bundle of letters. She stood up and pointed to the boxes. "I match the names and the apartment numbers."

"Don't talk to me like I can't understand simple things," Eddie said. "I may be crippled for a while, Barb, but I'm not dumb."

"I never thought you were," Barb said.

"Hand me my crutches," he ordered.

She gave them to him, and he used them to stand up. "What are you doing?"

"I can put up the mail," Eddie said, "faster than you can."

"You can not," Barb retorted.

"Watch me," Eddie said, and with one hand on the crutch for balance, he pushed letters into boxes with the other hand.

Barb's mouth fell open and she started to snap at him, then she grinned instead. Eddie was back! Good old Eddie, who tried to make everything between them a race.

She watched him stuff the mailboxes. Although she did it with a lighter touch, he may have been faster at it than she just because he wanted to beat her.

"Now you have to give it out to people, and you have to do it nicely," she said. "They all want mail, and not everyone gets something. I better do that part. You don't want to tire yourself by sitting up too long."

"I'm all right. I sat up lots of time in the hospital."

"What was it like?" Barb asked.

"It was bad," Eddie said as he sat down hard in the big desk chair. "But there were so many who were worse than me. Most of the kids were alone and didn't have their moms with them. I heard Mama say she couldn't have been there if it hadn't been for the hospital being shorthanded and Mrs. Burleigh recommending her."

"Mrs. Burleigh, our principal?"

"Yeah. Her brother runs the hospital, so Mama got special permission to stay with me, as long as she'd help with other patients, too."

That was news to Barb. She'd assumed all mothers could stay with their children. From down the hall she heard the distinct heavy footfalls that signaled Mrs. Hunter's afternoon trip to the office.

"Well, if it isn't Eddie back. You need me to work there so you can help him back to your apartment?" she asked.

"No, we're all right," Barb said. "No mail today, but here's the newspaper." She thought the woman would leave, but Mrs. Hunter leaned on the counter in front of the office window.

"How are you feeling, Eddie? You all right? Can you walk?"

41

"I can walk pretty good," Eddie said, although Barb knew that wasn't true. "Just need some practice."

"Well, take care of yourself," Mrs. Hunter said. She took the *Times* and settled herself on the couch.

"What happened to her?" Eddie whispered. He and Mrs. Hunter had never gotten on very well.

Barb shrugged. "You going to practice walking? Mama says you've got to get real good if you want to go to school on the first day."

Eddie winced. "I'll walk to the apartment and get a drink."

"We ought to set up a schedule of walking," Barb said. "Could you walk the entire hallway today? Then tomorrow you can do it twice. Then the next day three times." She could tell he was already tired from the excitement of coming home and sitting up for several hours, but wouldn't he do better if he had a goal?

Walking the halls became the plan. During the first week, Barb walked beside Eddie as he plodded along. Sometimes Warren came over, and he walked beside Eddie. Some days it was Carolyn who walked alongside him. Day by day, Eddie became stronger. Mama showed him how to take the stairs. There was a method of using crutches going down and a different way to use them going up. Eddie got good at it, but Barb never suggested a race. There would be no contest, and the knowledge that she would always win made her sad.

A week before school started, Barb and Eddie changed the exercise from the hallways to the regular walk toward school. Each day they made it farther before they'd turn around and go back to the hotel. Barb had to hand it to Eddie. He worked hard at walking, harder than she thought she'd ever be capable of working. Sweat broke out on his forehead sometimes, but he wouldn't give up. He kept walking.

Each afternoon, she and Eddie divided the mail and put it up. They talked of his disability, but Eddie was vehement that his leg was not permanently damaged. He said if he tried harder, he could make it well. At first Barb had agreed, but she had watched him gain strength in his arms from using the crutches, not strength in his bad leg. Now she didn't believe his leg would heal anymore than she believed Alice's fiancé would come back home.

By the first day of school, Eddie was ready. He had convinced Mama and Dad that he could make it, even though Aunt Daisy insisted on driving him the few blocks to school.

For the first time, Barb and Eddie weren't in the same classroom. Carolyn was in Miss Young's class with Eddie, and Warren was in Mrs. Counterman's class with Barb.

"I'll take care of him," Carolyn whispered to Barb as they stood in the hall reading the list of students in each room. "I'll treat him like he was my very own brother."

Barb started to object, but decided that maybe Carolyn needed a brother. Not that she was giving her twin away, but she was willing to share him with her friend.

Right after Mrs. Counterman introduced herself, she explained the air raid procedure. For the last two years, Dad had assured Barb over and over that the Japanese couldn't fly a plane close enough to shore to bomb them. But she remembered that radio program about the Germans launching buzz bombs from long distances away. If one of those came, then the students wouldn't even have time to get underneath their desks.

How was Eddie getting under his desk? He couldn't squat down like the rest of them. Surely his teacher was fixing some special place for him to be safe. At recess, Barb asked him, and he said they hadn't had air raid instructions yet, but he'd make sure his teacher found a place for him.

At one end of the playground, a group of boys played kick-ball. Barb, Carolyn, and Warren grouped around Eddie and talked about everything they could think of except the kickball game. Eddie kept glancing at the boys with the ball, and Barb saw a grim determination light his eyes. He shifted on his crutches when the ball got away from the boys and came straight at him.

"I can kick with my good leg," he said.

"You will not!" Carolyn exclaimed before Barb could object. But her words didn't keep Eddie from moving his weight to his bad leg and crutches and kicking the ball with his left foot. Because of his awkward angle, the ball only went a couple feet.

"A cripple can't play," Roy Madison called as he ran toward them for the ball.

"Ignore him," Barb said. She kicked the ball as hard as she could, and it sailed to the other end of the playground. Good. Roy could chase that silly ball.

"Roy's a creep," Warren said. "You need practice, that's all. Maybe we can borrow a kickball sometime and work on it."

"Mama says you can learn to walk without crutches. That ought to be first," Barb said.

Eddie immediately handed his crutches to Warren and took a few wobbly steps. Barb grabbed the crutches and propped him up. He seemed glad for the help.

"It'll just take practice," she said. "Look how fast you learned to walk with crutches."

"I'll put more weight on that leg every day. By the end of the month, I'll be playing kickball."

"Sure you will," Barb said, and she half-believed it. Sometimes she thought his leg would get better, and other days she knew it never would. She still prayed about it because Mama said she should.

The bell rang, calling the students back to the classrooms.

Eddie led the way and waved to Barb as he walked into Miss Young's room.

Mrs. Counterman handed out arithmetic books and assigned a page of twenty problems. A half hour later, she took up the papers and switched the subject to government.

"Because this is an election year, and since our government is in the forefront because of the war, we're going to have an election in our classroom. We'll elect a president, who will be in charge of our war stamp program. You will want to elect someone who has leadership skills and is a good organizer. Anyone who wants to run should pick up one of these forms, fill it out, and bring it back to school tomorrow." She held up several small sheets.

Barb glanced at the other students. Which one of the boys would make a good president? She didn't know all the boys in her class, but no outstanding candidate came to mind. She would make a better president. Barb sat up straighter in her desk. Why couldn't a girl be president? She knew how to organize. Hadn't she been keeping good records at the hotel office? Mama had told her last night that she'd like Barb to take a shift at the office after she got home from school.

She started to hold up her hand to ask if a girl could run, but thought better of it. She'd ask in private, after school.

The rest of the day passed slowly as Barb waited for her opportunity to get a form. When the last bell rang, she hung back as the other students rushed for the door. As she pretended to search her desk for something, she watched the teacher's desk out of the corner of her eye. Two boys picked up forms. When all students were out of the room, she walked to the desk and picked up a form.

"Is this just for boys?" she asked.

"Oh!" Mrs. Counterman said and looked a long moment at

Barb. "I guess a girl could run. Sure, why not? But you must be aware that your chances at being elected aren't as good as a boy's."

"I'm a good organizer," Barb said.

"I'm sure you are, but that has nothing to do with it. Students usually vote for boys, but that doesn't mean you won't get any votes. Give it some serious thought, Barbara. If you still want to run, turn in your form tomorrow. It would be interesting calling someone 'Madam President.' "

CHAPTER 5

The Elections

"I never heard of a girl president," Eddie said at supper that night.

"Does that mean there can't be one?" Barb asked.

"It sure doesn't," Isabel said. "A few years ago no one would have believed I could work at Boeing in production. Now there are lots of women who work on the line."

"But that's because of the war," Frank said. "Pass the potatoes, please."

"Girls are as smart as boys, aren't they, Dad?" Isabel asked.

Barb was glad she'd waited until suppertime to start this discussion about the school election. She wanted Isabel on her side.

"I'm not getting into this kind of argument," Dad said with a grin, "especially with your mother sitting here."

"If you want to be president, then you should go for it," Isabel said. "I don't know if you'd win, but you should run. I'll help you with your campaign speech."

"I don't know if we give speeches," Barb said. "But I could put up a banner like the one we made for Eddie."

"It's all right with me if you're a candidate," Mama said. She looked at Dad. "Any objections?"

"Not as long as she knows that her chances of winning are slim." He looked at Barb. "I don't want you disappointed."

"I won't be. I'm going to win," she said. At his frown, she added, "Aunt Daisy says to always have a positive attitude. So, I am." She handed the sign-up form to Frank, who passed it to Audrey, who passed it to Dad. "You have to sign it to indicate that you know the duties of the president include the war stamp collection."

The next day at school, Barb handed in her nomination form.

"Yours is the third one," Mrs. Counterman said. "I gave out three yesterday, so the race is on." She looked over the forms, and when the bell rang, she called the class to order. They said the Lord's Prayer and the Pledge of Allegiance, then Mrs. Counterman asked Barb, Tommy Brown, and Roy Madison to come to the front of the class.

"These three students are running for president of our class. We'll let them talk to the class tomorrow and answer any questions you may have, and then on Thursday we'll vote on our class president."

"What do we talk about?" Tommy asked.

"Why you would make a good president," Mrs. Counterman

said. "You don't have to give a long speech. A couple of minutes will do. You may be seated."

Barb walked to her desk and thought of reasons why she'd make a good president. She jotted her ideas down on paper so she could remember them when she was standing in front of the class tomorrow. Maybe this wasn't such a good idea after all. She'd never spoken to a whole group of kids.

"You'll do great," Carolyn said as they walked home from school.

Eddie had persuaded Mama to let him walk all the way home, so he limped on his crutches beside Warren. "Are you going to vote for Barb?" he asked. "I would if I were in her class."

Warren looked sideways at Barb and didn't commit himself. "Our class would be the only one with a girl president."

"We may be the only class with a president. Eddie's class isn't electing one," Barb said.

"Not yet," Carolyn said. "But I asked Miss Young if we were going to, and she said it might be a good idea."

At the hotel, Warren waved good-bye and walked on home, but Carolyn climbed the stairs and called her mom to see if she could stay awhile to work on Barb's campaign banner. Mama let Barb get a sheet before she took over office duties.

The girls were cutting out letters in the lobby when the postman came. Eddie sorted the mail.

"You got a letter from Steve," he said.

Barb put down her scissors and scurried to the desk. "I did? Just me?" Usually Steve's letters were addressed to the entire family. Only once had she received one addressed specifically to her. It had been a thank-you letter because she had sent him a bookmark she'd made in Sunday school. In carefully scrolled letters, she'd written a portion of the Twenty-third Psalm. The part about walking in the valley of the shadow of death, but fearing no evil, because God was with him. Steve was as big a hero in her eyes as her father, but she was afraid for him, and she didn't want him to be afraid.

Eddie handed her the letter and continued sticking letters in boxes.

Barb carefully opened it and scanned the contents. "He's using the code!" she exclaimed. "He wants a piece of pie. I think that means France. Eddie, get the code sheet from the drawer." He gave it to her, and she matched words and phrases. "He's written down what he wants for his first meal home. Translation: He was in Italy, then England, then in the D-Day invasion, and now he's in France."

The postmark was a month earlier, but Allied troops were still pushing across Europe toward Germany, so Steve was exactly where Dad had suspected. Knowing for sure made Barb feel closer to Steve. She wondered where in France, and decided her next letter would have code words for the big towns so she could pinpoint his exact location.

At supper that night, Barb showed off her banner and talked about her speech to Isabel, who gave her some pointers on how to speak to the class. Still, Barb had sweaty palms when it was speech time the next day.

"Ladies first," Mrs. Counterman said. Barb hid a frown. Isabel had told her to focus on how the candidates would organize and run the stamp drive instead of the boy-girl issue.

Barb walked to the front of the room and began. "My friends and classmates, I would be a good president because I've had experience organizing things. Over the summer I had a real job. I ran a hotel office during the afternoons." She listed her responsibilities. "I would use those skills to organize the war stamp drives. My brother Steve is in the army, and I work very hard on the home front to keep him safe. Please vote for me."

The class applauded. Next, Tommy spoke. He said he wanted to be president and would appreciate everyone voting for him. Roy mentioned the importance of war stamp sales in his speech.

"Any questions?" Mrs. Counterman asked. Barb was prepared for some, but no one raised a hand. "Tomorrow morning we'll have the election. It'll be by secret ballot, just like real elections, so no one will know how you voted. We'll count the ballots in class."

On the playground, when the teacher had walked back into the school, Roy sidled up to Barb. "Isn't your big hotel job in that place owned by the Japs?" He didn't wait for an answer before he said in a loud voice so other kids could hear, "She's running a Jap hotel!"

Barb was momentarily dumbstruck. Sure, the Wakamutsus were of Japanese ancestry, but they weren't the Japanese the United States was fighting.

"The owners came here before the war," she said. "They're on the American side."

"Sure they are," Roy said. "That's why the government locked them up."

Barb had no reply to that, but she asked Mama that afternoon when she was taking over the office.

"The Wakamutsus should never have been sent to the camp. Most of the Japanese would have become American citizens if they were allowed to. Yoshiko, Kaneko, and Abiko are Americans, born right here in Seattle."

"Then why were they locked up?" Barb said.

"I can't explain that. I think it was a big mistake made by people who are afraid of someone who looks different."

Barb nodded but didn't really understand.

The next morning at school, Barb hung her banner at the

front of the room. Neither one of the other candidates had made a sign.

"Are there any questions for the candidates before we vote?" Mrs. Counterman asked. She wrote three names on the blackboard, and each student voted for one on a small piece of paper. Barb voted for herself. Dad had said if she didn't have the confidence in her ability to lead, then she shouldn't be a candidate.

Mrs. Counterman carried a large jar down the aisles, and students dropped their ballots in it. She carefully mixed them up as if for a drawing, then she pulled one out at a time and read the name. With each name drawn, she put a tally mark by that candidate's name on the blackboard.

Barb held her breath as each name was read. She had won before the last few names were drawn. Of the thirty-two votes in her class, she already had eighteen before the final votes were read. That was more than half the class. Tommy ended up with seven, Roy had four, and Barb had twenty-one votes.

"Madam President, would you take over the meeting of the class?" Mrs. Counterman asked.

Barb walked carefully to the front of the room. Her heart felt as if it would burst inside her, and happiness washed over her. She had actually won, and won by a landslide. What a feeling!

She and Carolyn had planned what she would say if she won—and if she lost. Now she tried to remember. She should have brought her notes to the front with her.

"Thank you for electing me president. I'll do my best to do a good job. The first thing I'd like our class to do is make a banner for our room. We can use this sheet for the backing." She pointed to her campaign banner. "Would each one of you draw something that represents you or anything about you and sign it? We'll put the drawings on the banner."

"That's a fine idea, Barbara," Mrs. Counterman said. "Why

don't you think about what you will draw, and after arithmetic and reading, we'll make the banner."

At recess, Barb ran outside and told the others of her big win. "We're making the banner, just like we planned," Barb told Carolyn. It had actually been Isabel's idea. She said it would unite the class, and Carolyn and Barb thought it was a wonderful plan.

When Mrs. Counterman let them draw their objects for the banner, Barb drew a picture of the office at the hotel. She'd based her campaign on her experience there, so she thought it was fitting. Tommy drew a bicycle, since he rode everywhere. Roy drew a face with slanted eyes and big buck teeth, like in a newspaper cartoon, and then made a big X over it to show that the Japanese should be eliminated. Another student drew an airplane dropping bombs because his brother was a pilot. Still another drawing was of the American flag.

Each student pinned a drawing on the sheet until everyone was represented. Some of the drawings were not war related. A teddy bear, a baseball bat, a birthday cake, and a kickball found places on the banner.

Before they left school, Barb and Warren hung the banner above the door. Her next plan was to adopt a class mascot. Frank's high school had a wildcat as the mascot. Barb couldn't see the relationship to it and his school, but he said they were all wild and laughed. At the next weekly class meeting, when the war stamps were sold, she'd ask for suggestions.

Eddie's class was also going to hold an election. Barb urged her twin to run for president.

"Do you think they'd elect a cripple?" he asked. That was the first time Barb had heard Eddie call himself that, and she hoped it was the last time.

"You have one weak leg," she said. "And it's getting better."

She'd been helping him with exercises to strengthen it. Again they used the hotel hallways as practice areas, and he'd lengthened his walk each day. "I didn't think it would work again, but you've forced it to. You may have to wear the brace, but you won't need crutches much longer."

"But I'll always have a limp."

"What about President Roosevelt? He had polio, and he's the leader of our country. And I think he'll be elected again. Who could beat him?" She'd heard Dad say that just the night before.

With a little more persuasion, Eddie was convinced to run. Barb declared herself his campaign manager. Since he was helping in the office after school, he could use that job as a qualification in his speech. Carolyn and Warren helped them make a banner that said "Vote for Eddie."

On the day of the speeches, Eddie walked to the front of his classroom without his crutches. Barb wished she'd been there to see him, but Carolyn filled her in on every detail. When it was time for questions, Carolyn stood up and talked about how Eddie had worked hard to overcome polio and that he was a determined boy who would work hard for their class. Everyone applauded when she sat down.

The vote was between Eddie and one other boy, and although it was a close race, Eddie was elected president.

"The Harrington twins," Barb said at recess when she'd been told of Eddie's victory. "What a team!"

The twins fell into a routine. They worked together in the office after school, putting up the mail and giving it out. When there was no activity at the office, they did their homework. They planned their class meetings together, and Barb was very thankful that they were in different classrooms so they could both be presidents. She liked being in charge, and so did Eddie.

They continued Eddie's exercises, and he used his crutches

less and less. One evening in mid-September, he put away his crutches for good. Barb thought they ought to burn the crutches as a symbol of Eddie's triumph, but Mama said they'd better keep them. She splurged and bought a roast for dinner with meat stamps she'd been saving and said it would be a "good-bye to crutches" dinner. She invited Aunt Daisy to join the family. They were in a celebratory mood, but when Dad came home things changed.

"What's wrong?" Barb asked when she saw his grim expression.

"Bad news," he said. "Phil Johnson died." Barb had to search her memory until she remembered the name. Phil Johnson was president of Boeing, but he wasn't an old man.

"I didn't know he was sick," she said.

"He didn't know he was, either. He was in Wichita to check on the facility where they're making B-29s when a tumor in his brain started bleeding. It was all very sudden."

"What will happen at the plant?" Mama asked.

"I don't know who will move into his position. Work buzzed with speculation, but the outcome was that his death shouldn't change anything. Phil would have expected us to keep production going, but it won't be the same without him around."

The "good-bye to crutches" dinner became a "good-bye to Phil Johnson" dinner. Isabel had only met him once, but she told the story of shaking his hand when he came to the line. Dad remembered him as an intelligent man of vision.

"If there's one thing this war has taught us, it's how to deal with death," Aunt Daisy said. "We just give our dead to the Lord and somehow keep going."

Barb thought of Carolyn's brother and how hard it was on her family to let him go. She remembered the day her last year's teacher had found out that her husband's plane had been shot down over France. She thought of Jim Watson and how Alice still hadn't given up hope of his return. How would it all end? she wondered. And when would it all end?

As the days of fall slipped by, Barb followed the campaign for president of the United States. She listened to President Roosevelt's speeches and heard some of New York Governor Dewey's radio talks, too. She didn't have a doubt that Mr. Roosevelt would be reelected. He was president when she was born, and he was still president.

"He can't be too confident," Aunt Daisy said one day when she was picking up her mail. "Of course the Republicans are against him, but there are even some Democrats who think he's been president too long. Whoever heard of a man being elected to four terms? Of course, I'd hate to have a change of leadership in the middle of the war."

"He'll be elected," Barb said with confidence. She liked politics, she liked the people voting, and she liked President Roosevelt. Because he and Eddie had both had polio, she lumped them together in her mind.

She celebrated when election results were in and President Roosevelt was declared the winner. "He can lead us through the war," Barb said. "Maybe he'll even run a fifth time."

CHAPTER 6

The Battle of the Bulge

"Raymond's on Guam," Aunt Daisy said on Christmas Eve afternoon. She stood at the office window and read her son's letter out loud. When she finished, she folded the letter and held it to her heart. "Barb, let me look at that atlas again."

Barb was glad she'd carried the atlas to the office that afternoon. They'd been looking at it last night in their apartment after the latest news report on the Battle of the Bulge. The Germans had pushed the Allied front back sixty miles, and the American death count was very high.

Once again fear held a desperate grip on Barb's heart. Was Steve there? Was he okay? She knew he was in France earlier, and it seemed logical that he would be moving on toward Germany. Last night, Dad had pointed on the map to the town of Bastogne in Belgium.

When the Germans had demanded the surrender of the town, General McAuliffe had replied, "Nuts." Dad had said that was a gutsy thing to do, but the last news was that the town was still under siege. Was Steve holed up there? Or was he marching toward the town to fight?

She had carried the atlas to the office so she could look at the map again. Now she opened it to the Pacific islands and located Guam. "They must have sandy beaches and coconuts there," Barb said. What a contrast to the intense cold and snow that the reporter from Europe had mentioned in his live report on the radio last night.

"I wish we had developed more to that code," Aunt Daisy said. "Then I could know what Raymond was doing. He mentioned the sound of the airplane engines and nuts and bolts. Maybe that's a clue."

"Maybe he works on airplanes," Barb said. "Or maybe he rides in them and drops bombs." She had a sudden image in her mind of Japanese people on the ground running from falling buildings. She shuddered and moved her finger on the map from Guam to the Philippines, where Alice's fiancé had last been heard from.

"I'm sick of this war!" she exclaimed. She was stunned by her own words. They had boiled up from her heart and out of her mouth before she could think about them. "That's not patriotic, is it?" Barb asked. "I shouldn't have said that."

"I'm sick of it, too," Aunt Daisy said. "It has nothing to do with patriotism. It has to do with Christmas and peace on earth, and that's not what we're experiencing, is it?"

"No," Barb said simply. She looked at the Christmas tree in the lobby. She and Eddie had decorated it with the Wakamutsus' ornaments. The star at the top glistened, and colorful glass ball decorations hung from green branches. Steve didn't have a Christmas tree. He was probably in that dark European forest the radio news correspondent had described, shivering with the cold and wanting to be home for Christmas.

Aunt Daisy had turned to stare at the tree, too. "I guess Raymond's Christmas tree will be a palm tree. I doubt the army decorates barracks for holidays."

"No. I don't think soldiers have time to put up real Christmas trees," Barb said.

With a forced note of cheerfulness in her voice, Aunt Daisy said, "We miss them, but life goes on. Is everything ready for the party tonight?"

"I think so. Eddie and Frank are going to move tables out here around five. Mama didn't want to block the hallways too soon, but she wants everything set up before Dad gets home."

The party had been Barb's idea, and now she wished she'd never had it. Should they celebrate at home when friends and family couldn't be there?

"Barb, this is Christmas Eve. We have to get in a festive spirit," Aunt Daisy said.

"How can we when. . ." Her voice trailed off.

"It's time you faced your fear. What's the worst that can happen to them?" Aunt Daisy asked in a quiet voice.

"They could be killed."

"And then what?"

"We get the telegram that tells us they're dead."

"Yes, but what would happen to Steve and Raymond and the others?"

"They'd go to heaven."

"Exactly. That wouldn't be bad for them, now would it?"

Barb studied Aunt Daisy's eyes. In them she saw serenity and acceptance. Not the fear that was always in her own eyes.

"But what if they're tortured or die in terrible agony?"

"We pray that God will be with them." Aunt Daisy reached inside the office window and took Barb's hand. "You are too young to know all this fear. It doesn't help them. It only harms you. Now, give your fear to God, and He'll deal with it."

Barb closed her eyes and prayed that God would take her fear away. She opened her eyes and felt peace settle on her.

"Better?" Aunt Daisy said.

"Yes. Better," Barb answered.

"Good. Whenever you feel overwhelmed by fear, ask God to take it from you."

"How come you're so smart, Aunt Daisy?"

She smiled. "Because I lived with fear too long. I'm going to find your mother and see if she needs help."

The party was for everyone in the hotel. At seven, each person was to bring his own plate and silverware and one dish to share with the others. Mr. Lazarini from apartment four was going to bring his phonograph and some records. He mostly had operas, but Aunt Daisy had some Christmas albums she was going to bring, and Audrey had said she was going to guard her new Frank Sinatra record with her life and make sure it was played over and over.

The boys set up the tables early, confiscating as many as they could from residents in nearby rooms. Every room in the hotel was filled, but some people couldn't come to the party because of family gatherings and work shifts. Those who could make it wandered into the narrow lobby before the party officially began at seven.

Dad led the group in a prayer for the servicemen and in celebration for the birthday of Jesus. Then the merriment began. At least fifty people filled the narrow space, and all seemed to be talking at once. Even Mrs. Hunter, carrying dozens of cookies, came to the dinner party.

"I've been saving my sugar rations," she said, "so I could make my traditional Christmas favorites." She pointed to each kind. "These are date pinwheels. These white ones are Mexican wedding cakes, and these are my favorites, gingersnaps."

Barb put two cookies on her plate before she headed to the main food table loaded with chicken, potatoes cooked in a variety of ways, and lots of dishes of green beans.

Mr. Wiley struck up a conversation with Barb about his latest letter from his grandson. Because he had also used Barb's code, he knew that Tommy was in Belgium.

"He may be in that awful battle right now," Mr. Wiley said.

"Then may God be with him," Barb said and felt peace by saying it.

He nodded. "Yes, may God be with him."

Although several people lingered in the lobby talking, most had gone back to their own rooms by nine o'clock. Barb's brothers returned tables to their proper owners, and the girls picked up and swept and scrubbed the lobby. The entire area was cleaned up long before time to leave for the midnight church service, and the air of goodwill and cheer stayed with Barb.

The church was decorated in evergreen boughs and red bows. At the front sat a manger with real people representing the characters in the Christmas story. A tiny infant played the part of the baby Jesus. This year the baby slept through the whole performance and didn't cry once. Barb prayed for victory in Europe and in the Pacific and for peace all over the world.

When the Harringtons returned to the hotel, they opened

Christmas presents, which wasn't their tradition, but since Dad and Isabel had to be at work on Christmas morning, it seemed the best thing to do.

Barb received a wooden gavel from Dad, who said he was sorry he'd ever doubted that she would be elected president, a pocket-sized atlas, and a sweater. She went to bed tired, happy, and at peace for the first time in a long time.

The next day didn't seem like Christmas since Dad and Isabel were off to work before Barb got up. She and Eddie did their morning hotel chores, and that afternoon she again sat at the office while Mama worked on a Christmas feast for supper.

During the next week, news from the European front filled the papers. "What do you think of Patton's army entering Bastogne?" Mr. Wiley asked Barb one afternoon. "Pretty good, eh?"

Barb agreed and listened to his version of the Battle of the Bulge. Whenever fear edged into her mind, she forced it out by asking God to take it. The fear came less often, and she was able to talk about the battles and not worry that Steve might be fighting in them.

Just after the first of the year, Barb and Eddie were working in the office when a telegram came for Mr. Wiley. A deep foreboding enveloped Barb as she directed the delivery boy to Mr. Wiley's room.

"I'm going with him," Barb said. There had been too many stories told at school for her to think that a telegram meant anything but bad news.

She stood in the hallway and waited for Mr. Wiley to answer the messenger's knock. As soon as he saw the boy's telegraph uniform, Mr. Wiley's face turned a sickly white. He signed on the clipboard with a shaking hand and took the telegram. He was shutting the door when he looked up and met Barb's gaze.

"Come in," he said in a very low voice. He handed her the telegram. "Open this, please. My hands aren't steady."

Barb carefully opened the envelope. The message was as she suspected, except it was from Mr. Wiley's daughter and not the army.

"Sit down," she said. Instead of reading it aloud, she held it so he could see it.

His hand flew to his heart, and a groan escaped his lips. "No. . .no. . .no."

Barb found a glass and filled it with water. "Drink this, Mr. Wiley. I'm going to get my mother."

She hated to leave him, but she didn't know how to help him. With wings on her feet, she ran down the long hallway, around the corner, and down another hallway to the apartment.

"Mama! Mama!" she called as she opened the door. "Come quick. It's Mr. Wiley's grandson."

"Tommy's here?" Mama asked.

"No! Tommy's been killed in the war. Mr. Wiley needs you."

Mama dropped her mending and followed Barb back down the hallways to Mr. Wiley's room. He sat exactly where he had been when Barb had left him, only now his head was bowed and tears dripped onto his white shirt.

"I'm so sorry," Mama said. She picked up the telegram and read it. "Let's call your daughter from the office phone. She'll want to know that you received the news about Tommy and that you're with friends. She'll need your support, Mr. Wiley."

Barb carried Mr. Wiley's address book and held onto his arm as he walked between her and Mama down the hall.

"What's all the. . ." Mrs. Hunter had opened her door, looked at them, and then said, "Tommy?"

63

Barb nodded, and Mrs. Hunter backed into the room and shut the door.

By the time Eddie had moved out of the way and Mama had Mr. Wiley seated in the office chair, Mrs. Hunter stood at the office window, holding out a cup of hot tea.

"I already gave him water," Barb said.

"He needs a good strong cup of tea," Mrs. Hunter said and handed the cup through the window. Mr. Wiley took a sip, then drained the cup and took a deep breath. His color looked a little better.

Barb held Mr. Wiley's hand, or rather he held hers in a tight grip. Mama talked to the operator and gave the number for the long-distance call.

As soon as she had Tommy's mother on the line, Mama handed the phone to Mr. Wiley.

"Let's give him some privacy, kids," Mama said. Eddie and Barb edged around Mr. Wiley in the close quarters and followed Mama out the office door.

"The poor man," Mrs. Hunter said. "He thought the sun rose and set on that grandson of his."

"Tommy was always good about writing Mr. Wiley," Mama said. "I wonder where he was killed."

"Mrs. Harrington?" Mr. Wiley called from the office. Mama went inside while Barb and Eddie sat on the lobby couch by Mrs. Hunter. A few minutes later Mama and Mr. Wiley came out of the office.

"Barb, will you take Mr. Wiley back to his room?" Mama asked. "I have some calls to make."

Barb and Eddie escorted Mr. Wiley down the hall, with Mrs. Hunter leading the way. Once he was propped in his favorite upholstered chair, Mr. Wiley told them about Tommy, who had been killed on the second day of the Battle of the

Bulge. "And we're just now finding out," he said. "He's been gone nearly two weeks, and we're just now finding out."

"Tommy's a war hero," Eddie said.

"Yes, he is. He is," Mr. Wiley said.

They shared memories about Tommy, although Barb and Eddie had never met him. Barb looked at the framed photograph of Tommy that Mrs. Hunter held and remembered the stories Mr. Wiley had told her about this special young man.

A knock sounded on the door. Barb answered it and ushered Mama and Aunt Daisy inside.

"Your train leaves in two hours," Mama said. "Your daughter will pick you up in Albuquerque tomorrow afternoon. We'll help him get around, kids, so you can go back to the office."

Supper was delayed while Mama and Aunt Daisy took Mr. Wiley to the train station. "I hated leaving him alone on the train," Mama said. "But the conductor was looking after him. He needs to be with family."

"Did Mr. Wiley have the money for a trip?" Barb asked. From time to time he'd let slip that money was tight.

Mama glanced at Dad before she said, "Sometimes others step in when a friend needs help. Mr. Wiley needed to be with his family."

"I'm glad you helped him," Barb said. That night before she went to bed, she asked God to help Mr. Wiley, and she thanked Him that they hadn't received a telegram about Steve.

CHAPTER 7

The Wakamutsus Return

Eddie's limp was barely noticeable as he, Warren, Carolyn, and Barb walked home from school on a damp January afternoon. Their discussion centered on the war stamp sales, which were going well.

"At the end of the month, we'll do another count," Barb said. Her room and Eddie's room were both in the blue ribbon group on the sales chart. "My room may take over the lead by itself."

"Maybe, maybe not," Carolyn said. "Our room has a new plan to get more sales."

Barb raised her eyebrows. Eddie hadn't said anything about it, and he eventually told her everything, even if he tried to keep a secret.

They arrived at the hotel, and the group split up. As Barb and Eddie climbed up to the lobby, she asked him about the new plan.

Eddie didn't answer. Instead he stared at the office.

"Eddie?" Barb turned to look at what had him so fascinated, and her mouth dropped open in shock.

Mama and a Japanese woman stood in the office. It had been nearly three years since Barb had seen her, but the woman had to be Mrs. Wakamutsu.

The owners of the hotel were back! What would that mean? Would she lose the job she'd come to love? Sitting at the hotel desk had made her feel important. Now would they move back home to the house on Queen Anne Hill? Not long ago she'd wanted that, but now it would mean changing schools and giving up her position as president of her class, the only girl president in the entire school.

Barb hesitantly approached the office. Eddie seemed just as stunned as she was, for he hung back behind her.

A Jap in the office. A Jap. The word kept echoing in Barb's mind. What would Carolyn say? Oh, her friend had known they were running the hotel for a Japanese family, but somehow that knowledge and seeing a real Jap didn't fit together.

"Kids, come say hello," Mama said.

Barb and Eddie edged forward.

"Hello, little ones. My, how you've grown since I last saw you," Mrs. Wakamutsu said. "We've brought a surprise for you."

Could there be more of a surprise? Barb wondered. She finally found her voice and said hello. "When did you arrive?"

"We got here this morning, sooner than we expected. I wrote your mother, but we arrived before my letter." She laughed, a quiet sound. "We are so happy to be back home."

Home? Home! Where would they stay? There were no vacancies at the hotel. Surely they wouldn't expect Barb and her family to leave before nightfall.

"We've rearranged things a bit," Mama said. "You girls are all in one room now. It's wall to wall with five beds, but it will work for the time being."

Barb gazed silently at her mother. Five beds. She, Alice, Isabel, and Audrey made four, and there was only one set of bunks in that room. Barb was quite sure the Wakamutsus' only daughter had left the internment camp in the summer when she'd found a sponsor and a job in Chicago. Audrey had read that letter to her. Well, Yoshiko must have come back for a visit now that the Wakamutsus were free.

"Eddie, we've put Kaneko and Abiko in with you and Frank. The Wakamutsus will use the room Alice and Isabel shared." She turned to Mrs. Wakamutsu and hugged her. "I'm so delighted you're back."

"Do you want us to put up the mail?" Barb asked. Their normal routine was to put up their school things, get a glass of milk and a piece of bread, and report back to the office to relieve Mama before mail time.

"Sure," Mama said. "We've still got lots to do to get everyone settled in. Get a snack, and then you can take over." Barb turned to walk to the apartment when her mother called her back. "Oh, wait, the surprise." Mama scurried out of the office and walked with the twins down the hall.

The apartment was no longer a haven of peace and family love. Boxes were stacked in the middle of the living room so there was barely room to walk. Two Japanese boys were carrying boxes toward the bedrooms under the direction of Mr. Wakamutsu. Barb knew they had to be Kaneko and Abiko, but they had grown a foot taller since she'd last seen them.

Barb and Eddie exchanged greetings with the boys, and Mama called, "Yoko."

A young Japanese girl, about Barb's size, walked into the living room from the direction of the girls' bedroom.

"Here's the surprise," Mama said. "Yoko Muraro is staying with the Wakamutsus for a while. She'll be going to your school. Too bad she won't be in your class, since she's a grade younger."

Barb stared at the Japanese girl until Mama nudged her.

"Hello," Barb managed.

Yoko made a small bow in graceful Japanese fashion. "I'm so pleased to meet you," she said.

"You can introduce her around at school tomorrow," Mama said.

What was Mama thinking? Take a Jap to school? Be friends with a Jap? What would the other kids think? Oh, what about Carolyn!

"I'd better go back to the office," Barb said. "It's almost mail time."

"Yoko, would you like to join the twins in the office?" Mama asked.

Yoko looked at Barb and said, "Perhaps in a little while. I am still unpacking."

"Of course," Mama said.

Barb skipped her usual after-school snack and hurried back to the office, carrying her schoolwork with her.

69

"You may go back to the apartment if you wish," she told the Japanese woman at the office. "Yoko is still unpacking."

"Yes, we have lots to do," Mrs. Wakamutsu said. "We are storing some boxes in the linen room. How could we have accumulated so much during our stay at the camp?"

Barb smiled but didn't comment.

"Barbara, I hope you will be kind to Yoko. Her mother died two years ago, and her father is in the army. He has entrusted her to our care until he returns. If he returns."

Barb nodded but didn't promise anything. Mrs. Wakamutsu left the office, and Barb sat down with a sigh of relief. What was happening to her world? Just when she had gotten settled, something else happened to disrupt her life.

Eddie opened the office door.

"What do you think?" Barb asked without explaining any further.

"I'm glad she's not a boy. You get to take her around school and not me. Why is she here?"

Barb explained the little she knew about Yoko. "I feel sorry for her, but she's a Jap."

It felt odd to say that out loud. It felt wrong, yet kids at school said it all the time. Get the Japs. Kill the Japs.

"Mail here yet?" Mrs. Hunter was at the window as was her habit this time of day.

"He's running a little late," Barb said. She held out the newspaper. "The Wakamutsus are back."

"I know. I saw them move in this morning." She shrugged. "It's nothing to me. I rented from them, but I've heard talk that some of the new residents. . .aren't pleased." She said the last as if she were searching for the right words. "After all, if Roosevelt thought they were a threat and had them locked up, aren't they still a threat? That's what I've heard people say." She lumbered over to the couch and sat down with the paper.

Mrs. Hunter had a point. Barb didn't know much about the lock-up order, but she was going to ask questions. But who could she ask? She might not get any time alone with Mama and Dad without the Japs around.

There it was again. It didn't feel right thinking of the Wakamutsus as Japs. She had thought of them as the Japanese family her parents were helping out while they were in the relocation center. But talk at school was about Japs in America being spies. That's why they had been sent to the camps.

The mailman delivered a large packet of letters. Eddie took half, and Barb took half.

"Here's a letter from Mr. Wiley," Eddie said. "It's to Mama and Dad. And here's the one from the Wakamutsus."

"Nothing from Steve in my pile," Barb said.

"Nothing here, either," Eddie said, "but here's a letter from Raymond."

Of course, Aunt Daisy—that's who she could ask about the Japs. Barb could ask her anything. "I'll deliver it. Can you take care of the office by yourself?"

Eddie looked at her with his "who do you think you're talking to" look.

"Sorry. I'll be back in a few minutes."

Barb scurried down the hall to Aunt Daisy's apartment. Once inside, she impatiently waited while Aunt Daisy read her son's letter before bombarding her with questions.

"He was still on Guam when he wrote this," Aunt Daisy reported. "I wonder if he went to the Philippines. There was bad fighting in Luzon."

71

"It doesn't do any good to worry about him," Barb said. "Face your fear. What's the worst that could happen?"

Aunt Daisy smiled. "Didn't I give you this lecture?"

"Yes, and it helped me."

"And it helps me when fear rears its ugly head," Aunt Daisy said. "What's bothering you now? You've got that look." She reached over and smoothed the line between Barb's eyebrows. "If you scrunch up like that whenever you have a problem, you're going to have some big wrinkles."

Barb moved over by the mirror beside the door and looked at her reflection. Sure enough, she had a scrunched-up look. "Eddie looks like this when he's worried."

"Twins do that. Even if they aren't identical, they have some of the same habits. So what's bothering you?"

Barb walked back to a chair across from Aunt Daisy and announced, "The Wakamutsus are back."

"I know."

"They're Japs."

"Yes, they are."

Didn't Aunt Daisy understand? "Raymond's fighting the Japs. Doesn't that bother you? Don't you hate them?"

"Yes, I hate them. But we're not fighting the Wakamutsus. They've lived here for many years. Their children were born in Seattle. That makes them American citizens."

"Then why were they sent to camps?"

Aunt Daisy pursed her lips. "That's a good question, and I don't have a good answer because I don't understand it myself."

"Didn't President Roosevelt send them to the camps?"

"He signed the order, but I imagine there was a lot of pressure brought on him by people who were afraid. See, Barb, fear makes people do some crazy things." Aunt Daisy explained about the removal of the Japanese to the inland camps and the new order letting them return to coastal cities like Seattle.

"Couldn't they prove they weren't spies?"

"I don't think they were given the chance. The thought was that most of them have relatives in Japan. They would have to have divided loyalties. You ought to talk to Mrs. Wakamutsu about this."

"I can't ask her!"

"Why not? I imagine she'd be very interested in your reaction. She's going to get it a lot. People are still fearful. They act badly when they're afraid."

"She brought a Japanese girl with them. I have to take her to school tomorrow."

"Oh, so that's what all this is about."

"All the kids hate the Japs."

"So, tomorrow could be a hard day."

"Very hard."

"You're the only girl president in the school, Barb. You're a leader. You can figure out a way to make the students accept this girl."

"How?"

Aunt Daisy smiled again, a sly smile. "I don't know, but you're a bright girl. You'll figure it out."

That wasn't the answer Barb wanted, and she muttered to herself as she walked down the hall to the office. How would she handle tomorrow? What would Carolyn do when she met Yoko?

That evening the Harringtons and the Wakamutsus had a grand dinner. There wasn't room for everyone at the dinner table, so the younger kids carried their plates to the living room to eat. An air of festivity dominated the small apartment. Barb tried to get into the mood, but she felt as if a cloud the size of the one that normally blocked the top of Mount Rainier hung over her.

Yoko asked Barb some questions about school, and she answered them the best she could.

"You'll have to go to the principal's office, and she'll tell you which class you'll be in. Mrs. Swain's class is one of the smallest, so I think you'll end up there." That class was always at the bottom of the stamp sale list because it didn't have as many kids to buy stamps.

As soon as everyone had eaten, the two families crowded into the living room for a meeting. Every chair was taken, and the floor was covered with kids, some sitting on unopened boxes.

"You all know the sleeping arrangements," Dad said. "As soon as there are vacancies in the hotel, we'll spread out. But for now this will have to do. We signed a contract with the families who rented our house, so we can't move back home until the first of June. That will let you kids finish the school term here."

Barb breathed a sigh of relief. At least she could still be president.

"We had a letter from Mr. Wiley today." Dad explained to the Wakamutsus that Tommy had been killed in the war. "He's going to move in with his daughter in New Mexico. We'll crate up his things and ship them to him. As soon as that's done, there will be one room available to us.

"The Wakamutsus will gradually take over running the hotel, but we'll be assisting them until they get things unpacked and can reassign chores. That will give Mama more time to work on the ration board and other volunteer work. Any questions?"

"What about after school at the office?" Eddie asked.

"You and Barb can keep putting the mail up for the time being," Mama said.

That was another relief. Doing her homework in the office was much better than coming to this cramped apartment to find a space to sit down. Maybe when they were moved to other hotel rooms, things would get better.

"Any other questions?" Dad waited, but no one spoke up. "Then I'd like us all to bow our heads to thank God for the Wakamutsus' return."

Dad ended his prayer with the usual request that the war would soon end and that Steve, Jim Watson, Raymond, and the other soldiers would return home. This time he included Harry Muraro, Yoko's father, in his prayer.

The bedroom was crowded, and it took Barb awhile to get to sleep on the hard cot. Yoko's cot was only inches from hers. Before sleep claimed her, the thought crossed Barb's mind that the little Jap could stab her in her sleep. She pushed the thought away. This was that ugly fear again. Yoko was an American. Her father was fighting in the war. Surely that would overrule her Japanese blood.

The next morning, Barb trudged alongside Yoko as they walked to school. Eddie had left early to set up a special stamp sale exhibit, the new plan Carolyn had mentioned the day before. Barb figured he didn't want to be seen with Yoko.

Barb took Yoko to the office and waited as Mama had told her to while Yoko was assigned a teacher. Then Barb walked her to her classroom and introduced her to Mrs. Swain. At recess, she saw Yoko standing by herself on the playground and forced herself to go over to her.

"Come meet my friend," Barb said and took Yoko to where

Carolyn was talking with another girl.

"Carolyn, this is Yoko Muraro. She's living with us at the hotel."

Carolyn took one look at Yoko, glared at Barb, then turned and stormed off.

CHAPTER 8

Yoko's Story

Barb was ignored by Carolyn the entire day. When it was time to go home, Carolyn didn't walk out of Miss Young's classroom with Eddie.

"Where's Carolyn?" Barb asked.

"She said she had something to do after school," Eddie said and nodded back at the room.

Barb stuck her head in his classroom and saw Carolyn standing by her desk as if waiting for something. "Coming?"

"No. Traitor!"

Barb recoiled as if she'd been hit. How could Carolyn call her a traitor? She couldn't help it that President Roosevelt had let the Japs out of the camps. Well, if that's the way Carolyn wanted it, fine.

Barb marched back to where Eddie had been joined by Yoko. "Let's go. Where's Warren?"

"He went with Jack Bloome," Eddie said.

"Oh," Barb said. So Eddie was also being treated badly because of Yoko. "Well, let's get home." Home? "Let's go to the hotel," she corrected herself. Maybe it was a good idea for them to go back to the house on Queen Anne Hill. Anywhere would be better than this.

"Your friends are not kind," Yoko said once they were on the sidewalk.

"They don't understand," Eddie said. "We've been at war against the Japs a long time."

"I am not a Jap. I am an American." Yoko said it with quiet authority that made her seem old. "I was born in California. My father is Nisei, born in California. My grandfather was Issei, born in Japan, but that was a long time ago. Long before the war."

"But you look Japanese," Barb said.

"That is my heritage, but Japan is not my country." Yoko said it with such sincerity that Barb believed her.

"It will be hard to convince the kids at school about that," Eddie said.

"I know," Yoko said. "They call me a Jap, but I am not the enemy. They need to know me, not just the way I look."

They had arrived at the hotel, but Barb held back from climbing the stairs. It would be hard to talk frankly with Mama and Mrs. Wakamutsu around, and Barb wanted to know more about Yoko. The girl fascinated her in an odd way.

"We want to know you, but it's hard to look past your yellow skin and slanted eyes," Barb said honestly.

"Then I feel sorry for you," Yoko said. "You are blind."

First she'd been called a traitor by Carolyn, and now Yoko had called her blind. They were both wrong.

Barb stomped up the stairs. She rushed to the apartment that looked even worse than yesterday. Boxes were opened and half unpacked. Barb glanced at the table where her great-great-grandmother's wooden clock had set. It was gone, and in its place stood a gnarled miniature tree, maybe a foot tall, in a flat green planter. It looked like it belonged in an enchanted forest with its thick trunk and spreading branches.

"Where's the clock?" Barb asked no one in particular, although Abiko, Frank, and Audrey were in the living room. They'd obviously just returned from school, too.

"I don't know," Audrey said. "What is this beautiful tree?"

"Bonsai," Abiko said. "It is Yoko's. Her father inherited it from his grandfather, who inherited it from his father and his father before him. It is very old."

"Then it is Yoko's father's tree," Barb said.

"Yes, but he is at war." Abiko added matter-of-factly, "He will not return."

"Why not? Is he missing in action?" Barb knew in her heart that Jim Watson wouldn't return, but he had not been officially declared dead—just missing in action because the navy didn't know what had happened to him.

"No. But when a soldier goes off to war, he does not expect to return."

"Yes, he does," Barb said. "Steve's coming back."

Abiko shrugged. "A soldier fights to his death. It is the honorable thing to do."

Barb had no reply. She got a drink and then went to the

office to relieve her mother and Mrs. Wakamutsu, who were going over the books.

"We need to work here a bit longer," Mama said. "Then I must make a few more calls for the March of Dimes. Why don't you and Yoko walk down to the drugstore and get something special to drink? You can show her the neighborhood." She handed Barb some change. "Barb, I'd like you to be kind to Yoko. She needs a friend."

Barb nodded. Now what could she do? She went in search of Yoko and found her in the girls' bedroom. She sat primly on her cot holding Mittens, Yoshiko's cat that Isabel had adopted when the Wakamutsus were forced to leave for the camps. Yoko petted it with loving strokes.

"Mama says we should walk to the drugstore."

"You do not have to," Yoko said.

"Yes, I do. Mama said to."

"Of course, you must honor your mother's wishes." Yoko slipped on her shoes, and Barb led the way out of the hotel.

"You have to stay away from the burlesque house. It's not a nice place." Barb pointed out the obvious sites as they walked down the street: the café, the barber shop. Two blocks farther down the street was the drugstore. Barb held the door for Yoko.

"After you," Yoko said in that cultured tone of hers.

"Go on. I've got the door," Barb said.

"Thank you," Yoko said with a nod of her head.

They sat at a small table next to the window and ordered Coca-Cola. It was a treat for Barb to be there, but the odd looks she was getting from other customers because of Yoko took the shine off the special feeling of being independent.

"I'm sorry I said you were blind," Yoko said.

"That's okay," Barb said. "I'm not blind. I'm not a traitor, either."

"I did not say you were."

"No, but Carolyn did."

They drank their Cokes without talking until Barb couldn't stand the silence. "So what was it like in the camp?"

"It was like a town, except we lived in large barracks. My family had one small room next to the Wakamutsus' room. Outside was dusty and so cold in the winter. We had to walk to a big hall to eat bad-tasting food."

"What did you do all day?"

"I went to school. Like here, except we were all yellow-skinned, not white. No one pointed at me and called me a Jap."

"When did your mother die?" It came out more abruptly than Barb intended, but she wanted to get Yoko off the subject of how she'd been treated at her first day of school in Seattle.

"Over two years ago. November 30, 1942."

"She died in the camp?"

"Yes. She had pneumonia. She was very pretty, even at the end."

"Where is she buried?"

"In Idaho. We had to leave her there." Tears glistened in Yoko's eyes. Barb searched for another subject.

"What about your father?"

Yoko sniffed. "He's in the 442nd. Have you read about them in the paper?"

"No."

"There are many clippings about the bravery of the Nisei Combat Team. I will show them to you. My father is a brave soldier."

If Yoko's father was a soldier, didn't that prove that he was a loyal American? Barb would get those clippings and show them to Carolyn. Yoko's family wasn't her brother's enemy. Yoko's family was fighting to avenge Carolyn's brother's death. Once Carolyn understood that, surely they would be friends again.

"Do you like Frank Sinatra?" Barb asked, changing the subject once again, this time to a neutral topic. "My sister is crazy about his music."

"I have heard him on the radio," Yoko said. "He sounds nice, but I am not crazy for him."

"Me, either," Barb said. "Hey, did you see the movie *Bataan*? My sister's fiancé was on the Philippines when it was taken by the. . ." She'd started to say Japs, but corrected herself. Even though Yoko wasn't one of them, she was still of Japanese descent. "Anyway, Alice has seen that movie five times and cried through it every time."

"I would like to go to the movies," Yoko said.

"Sometimes Eddie and Warren and Carolyn and I go on Saturday afternoons. *Meet Me in St. Louis* is playing now. I'll ask Mama if we can go this Saturday." And before then, Barb determined that she'd explain everything to Carolyn.

The girls left the drugstore and walked back by a different route so Yoko could learn more of the neighborhood.

The next day at school, Carolyn again ignored Barb. It rained during recess, so everyone stayed in classrooms for games instead of going outside. Barb only saw Carolyn once, and that was when Barb and Eddie went from room to room to tell about the March of Dimes drive. The principal had selected them to announce the campaign against polio because of Eddie's brush with the disease. Carolyn didn't even look at Barb when Barb read to the class the information about mothers collecting dimes for polio research.

Eddie talked briefly about having polio and said that he was one of the lucky ones. Many others in the hospitals were in wheelchairs or would always walk with crutches or had died. Barb was surprised when he lifted his pants leg to show his brace. Some of the boys had ridiculed him about it when school had first started, but now it was like a battle wound. He had survived polio. He was a hero.

In her short speech, Barb said that polio research needed to be done right away so that someone else in school didn't get the disease next summer. She saw fear in the eyes of some students and thought that Aunt Daisy would approve of that fear if it got more dimes in the bucket for research.

After school, Carolyn had left the building before Barb made it to Eddie's room.

Barb and Eddie put the mail up after school, but Mama needed the office phone for last minute calls about the March of Dimes, so she took over. The whole month of January was March of Dimes month, but the next day Mama would collect dimes in the neighborhood, and other mothers on her list would walk their areas, too.

"I will also collect dimes," Mrs. Wakamutsu said. "This is a cause for all of us. Next summer could be a worse year for polio. We do not want Yoko or Barb to get the disease."

Barb had thought the fear of the disease was good for the kids at school, but she didn't like it linked to herself. She remembered those horrible days last summer when first thing every morning she had checked her fingers and toes to make sure they still worked.

"We should make a lot of money for the March of Dimes," Mama explained to Mrs. Wakamutsu. "The whole country is behind the effort. When a movie star like Mary Pickford can take time to be the honorary head of the women's drive, then you know we'll have a successful collection. Last week Jack Benny mentioned the drive on his radio show." She laughed. "If a skin-flint like him is going to donate a dime, then everyone should."

"We listened to his funny show at the camp," Mrs. Waka-mutsu said. "Yoshiko sent us a radio after she got her job."

Since Mama didn't need her at the office, and she didn't have homework, Barb asked if she could walk over to Carolyn's.

"Be home before five. Would you like Yoko to go with you?"

"No," Barb said. "I need to talk to Carolyn alone."

Barb didn't call Carolyn before she walked over. If Carolyn knew she was coming, she might go somewhere. Barb dreaded the confrontation, but she wanted things worked out between them. It was time to face her fear, as Aunt Daisy would say. Carolyn had been too good a friend to desert just because she didn't understand that Yoko wasn't a real Jap. She just looked like one.

Carolyn's mother opened the door and invited Barb inside. "Carolyn's in her room doing homework," she said. "I'll get her."

Barb walked over to the piano and looked at the display of photographs in various-sized frames. There were Carolyn's parents in their wedding portrait and another photo taken in their wedding attire with their parents on each side, a family portrait of Carolyn with her parents and her brother, Carolyn's grand-parents beside a sign that Barb couldn't read since it was in a foreign language, one of Kenneth in his navy uniform before that awful day at Pearl Harbor, and several old school pictures of Carolyn and Kenneth.

"What are you doing here?" Carolyn asked the moment she came in the room. Her voice was low, probably so her mother wouldn't hear her being rude.

"Just looking at pictures," Barb said. "Aren't these your grandparents?"

"Yeah, so?"

"Where was this picture taken?" Barb had a good idea of the location, but she had to get Carolyn to say for sure.

"When they went to Europe."

"What country were they in? I can't make out the writing on this sign." Barb picked up the photograph. "It looks like German."

Carolyn's glance at Barb was lightning fast, but Barb saw the suspicion in her eyes. "So?"

"Why did they go to Germany?"

"That's where my grandfather was born," Carolyn said, "but he came to this country when he was only three years old. He went back to see what it was like."

"Then you're a Nazi," Barb said.

"I am not! That's the stupidest thing you've ever said, Barbara Harrington."

"Is your father in the army?"

"No, but neither is yours."

"Yoko's father is. Her grandfather was born in Japan, but came here when he was a young man. Her father was born in California, and so was she. She's not a Jap. She's as American as you are."

Carolyn was silent for a moment.

"But she looks like a Jap."

"And you look like a German." Barb touched Carolyn's blond hair.

"Why was she sent to the prison camp if she's not a Jap?"

"I don't know. Aunt Daisy thinks it was fear because she looked like the enemy, but sending Yoko's family to the camp wasn't called for. It was a mistake," Barb said. "Her mother died there," she added to make Carolyn view Yoko with more sympathy. "They buried her in Idaho. Yoko can't even go put flowers on her grave."

Carolyn frowned and looked thoughtful. "We can't go to Kenneth's grave, either, since he's buried on that ship in Pearl Harbor. I need to think about this."

"Me, too," Barb admitted. She wouldn't push Carolyn, because she knew her friend would come to the right conclusion. "You want to ask your mom if you can go with us to the movie on Saturday?"

CHAPTER 9
The Plan Backfires

That evening Barb was quite pleased with herself for convincing Carolyn that Yoko was an American instead of the enemy. Barb felt sure that Carolyn believed that now, even though she hadn't actually said it. But when Barb went to school the next day, there were two Japanese boys in her own classroom, and most of the class snubbed them. Only Barb and one other boy, Nick Mensetti, went out of their way to talk to the boys.

Mrs. Counterman had the Japanese boys draw something for the class banner. Before going outside with the rest of the class for recess, Barb climbed on a chair and pinned on the two new drawings. The only spaces left were right next to the one of the big X over the buck-toothed Jap.

On the playground, Barb saw Eddie playing kickball. He'd set his mind on playing that game, and he'd made it happen. He'd taken the other kids' attitudes and turned them around. Instead of ridiculing his impairment, now they admired him for overcoming it.

The two Japanese boys from her classroom stood off to themselves instead of joining in a game with the others. A lone Japanese girl stood by the fence. Thankfully it wasn't Yoko. Carolyn was actually talking to her over by the swings.

Something had to be done to make others accept the Japanese, but what? The country was at war with the Japs. Barb's classmates had worked hard to raise money to fight the Japs, and now she expected them to welcome yellow-skinned, slant-eyed classmates? She couldn't erase their hatred for Japs as easily as she had convinced Carolyn to talk to Yoko. Or could she?

Barb walked with purpose back into the school and found Mrs. Counterman at her desk grading arithmetic tests. She explained her idea to her teacher, who looked thoughtful, then said it was worth a try.

As soon as the kids were called in from recess, Mrs. Counterman began the social studies lesson.

"Yesterday we talked about the potato famine forcing a great many Irish to immigrate to the United States. Does anyone have an ancestor who was Irish?" Three or four students held up their hands. "Did any of your grandparents or great-grandparents come to this country in the late 1840s?"

This time there were no hands raised. Finally Kathleen O'Sullivan spoke up. "I don't know when my father's parents came here, but we celebrate St. Patrick's Day every year."

"That's a fun celebration," Mrs. Counterman said. "We all

like wearing something green on March 17, even if we don't have a drop of Irish blood."

"My mom has a shamrock plant," Casey Malone said.

"Good," Mrs. Counterman said. "That's another thing we associate with the Irish. Are any of you from England?"

Barb held up her hand along with a smattering of others.

"My ancestors came over on the *Mayflower*," Barb said with pride. "They were Pilgrims."

"Can others of you trace your family back to the first colonies?" Mrs. Counterman asked.

No one held up a hand.

"Jeff, do you know when your family came here from England?" Mrs. Counterman asked.

"No, but maybe I could find out."

"That's a great idea. Would each one of you find out who your ancestors were and where they came from and when they came to this country? If your parents don't know, perhaps you can ask your grandparents. We'll each share our stories in social studies tomorrow."

Barb told her idea to Eddie, Yoko, and Carolyn as they walked home from school. "Tomorrow everyone will tell how many generations they have been in this country. Then they will see that we're all Americans."

"Good. Maybe then Warren will walk home with us," Eddie said.

"Have you talked to him?" Barb asked.

"No. He won't talk. He just plays with the other boys at recess. Where did he go after school?"

"Sorry, I didn't notice, but I will tomorrow. I'll ask him if he wants to go to the movie with us on Saturday. How's that?"

"Okay," Eddie said and scurried on ahead of the girls.

He was already alone in the office when Barb and Yoko climbed the stairs to the lobby.

"Mama and Mrs. Wakamutsu are doing the March of Dimes," he said. "Alice was working here when I came in."

The mailman clomped up the stairs early and handed a bundle of letters to Eddie.

Barb wanted to follow Yoko to the apartment for a drink, but she went inside the office instead. Sorting the mail kept her in the know about what was going on in the hotel.

"Oh, no," Eddie said. He handed Barb a letter for Mr. Wiley.

Barb read the return address and gasped. "A letter from a dead soldier. Oh, I wonder when Tommy wrote this."

She figured that Mama would send it on to Mr. Wiley, whose things had been shipped to Albuquerque the day before. Today his room was to be cleaned, top to bottom, and Alice and Isabel were moving in there that night.

There was no letter from Steve and, of course, no letter from Jim Watson for Alice, but Aunt Daisy had two letters from Raymond.

Once they had put up the other mail, Barb took the letters and dashed down the hall to Aunt Daisy's apartment. She wanted to tell her how she had convinced Carolyn that Yoko was a loyal American and all about the social studies project.

Once again Barb waited while Aunt Daisy read her son's letters.

"Well, he was still on Guam when he wrote these letters. They were written a week apart, but delivered the same day. Hard to figure how the mail system works in a war zone," Aunt Daisy said and refolded the second letter, just as she had the first. Barb knew she would read them again and again, then put them with the others.

"Carolyn and Yoko are friends," Barb announced. "Well, maybe not friends like Carolyn and I are, but they're not enemies anymore." She explained how she had managed to get Carolyn to accept Yoko and also shared her plan for the social studies class. "I told them my ancestors came over on the *Mayflower*," Barb said proudly. "No one else could trace their families that far back."

"Did you also mention your mother's father?"

"I never knew my grandfather. He died before I was born."

"Your mom's told me a bit about him. You must ask her about him before you go to school tomorrow."

"I will. I'll ask Dad about his parents, too."

"Oh and, Barb, don't get too uppity about your family coming over on the *Mayflower*. My family met them on the shore."

"What are you talking about?"

"As Will Rogers said. . . Oh, you wouldn't know him, but he was a famous man from Oklahoma. Anyway, he said that his people met the boat." Aunt Daisy laughed. "I'm part Indian. My great-grandmother was Cherokee. I'm not sure what tribe lived around Plymouth Rock, but I suspect I'm related somewhere back there. I can trace my ancestors back to the first Americans. So to my family, your old, old family members were recent immigrants."

Barb nodded, and Aunt Daisy was still chuckling when Barb left her apartment. Odd, Aunt Daisy didn't look like an Indian. Oh, her hair was dark all right, but she wasn't real tall, and she didn't have red skin.

Barb stayed at the office where Eddie was giving out mail and talked to him about the ancestor assignment, urging him to do the same thing in his room. There were no Japanese in his class right now, but there were bound to be some soon. All the internment camps were being closed down, little by little.

After supper that night, Barb cornered her dad and asked about his family. With her pencil in hand, she made notes in her social studies notebook.

"Slow down," she said. "Your mother was from New York and your father from Minneapolis. But where did they come from originally, like Mama's family is from England."

"South Africa."

"South Africa!"

"It's part of the British Commonwealth. I'm sure my ancestors at one time came from England, but I don't know when they immigrated to South Africa and then came to America. That's on my father's side. On my mother's side, I think there's some Dutch heritage, but that's way back there."

"Thanks. Where's Mama?"

"She just got back from the big march and is in Mr. Wiley's room helping sort out the girls' things. This move will give you girls some much-needed room. I was sent to get a hammer so I can hang a few pictures."

Barb tagged along down the hall to Mr. Wiley's room, now filled with Alice's and Isabel's belongings. Mama was hanging up dresses.

"Can we talk about my homework, Mama?" Barb asked. "I need to find out about our ancestors."

"Fine, dear. What do you want to know?" Her muffled voice came from the built-in closet, another of father's improvements to the hotel.

"I know our ancestors came over on the *Mayflower*. Was that on your mother's side or your father's side or both?"

"Mother's side."

"What about your father's side?"

Mama turned around to face Barb. "It's too bad Grandpa Schmidt died before you were born. You would have liked him. You have a lot in common."

"Schmidt? That doesn't sound like an English name."

"Because it's not. It's German."

No! Barb thought. *This can't be true.*

"My father came from Germany when he was a boy."

Barb stepped back. What was her mother saying? That Barb's grandfather was a German?

"But Steve is fighting the Germans," Barb said.

"He's fighting the Nazis," Mama said. "Honey, haven't you heard us talk about the way German Americans were treated during World War I? No," she answered her own question, "I guess you were pretty young when Audrey asked so many questions about it."

"But, Mama, we can't be German," Barb protested.

"You are part German, and it's a heritage to be proud of," Mama said with an edge to her voice. "The Germans are a hard-working people."

Barb looked down at her social studies notebook. She had been so proud that her people had come over on the *Mayflower*, but she added German to the list.

The next day at school, Barb met Carolyn at recess before Yoko came outside.

"My grandfather was German," Barb blurted out. She'd struggled with the idea of keeping it a secret, but that wouldn't be fair to Carolyn after she had sort of tricked her into accepting Yoko as an American. Aunt Daisy always said, Face your fear, and that was exactly what she was doing.

"What?" Carolyn asked, although Barb was quite sure she'd heard her.

"I thought you should know that my Grandpa Schmidt came over from Germany, too."

"So we both have ancestors in Germany that we're fighting against," Carolyn said.

"I guess so. I'll bet there are others in my class who didn't know they had German ancestors."

"But they may not tell it," Carolyn said.

"I didn't want to tell you," Barb admitted.

Yoko joined them, so they dropped the subject and played a game of hopscotch before recess was over.

"Okay, class, it's time for social studies," Mrs. Counterman said when Barb was back in class. "I hope you asked your parents about your ancestors. Who wants to go first? I'll write the different countries on the blackboard."

Roy Madison held up his hand. "My dad's family is from England and my mom's is from England, too."

"When did they come to America?" Mrs. Counterman asked.

"A long time ago, but they don't know when," Roy said.

"All right." She wrote "England" on the board. "Johnny?"

"Both my parents are from England, but I don't know when they came here."

This wasn't going according to Barb's plan. Were all the kids going to say they came from England? As much as she didn't want to do it, she held up her hand.

"Barb?"

"Well, I told everyone yesterday that my ancestors came over on the *Mayflower,* and they did. But that was just on my mother's mother's side. On my dad's mother's side, they are Dutch people. On my dad's father's side, they came from South Africa."

There were low "oohs" from some students after Barb

mentioned that exotic location. She explained about South Africa belonging to England at one time.

"My mom's father was from Germany."

"Germany!" Roy Madison spat out the name with disgust.

"He came over when he was a boy," Barb said defensively. "He was a hard-working German, but he wasn't a Nazi!" If she could have, she would have busted Roy right in the nose for making this confession so hard.

"Of course, he wasn't," Mrs. Counterman said. "Nick Mensetti, where are your ancestors from?"

"My mama's family is from England, but I don't know when they came over. And my papa's family is from Italy. Papa came over from Italy when he was ten."

"Fascist!" Roy Madison exclaimed.

Nick jumped to his feet with his fist raised.

"That's enough, Roy," Mrs. Counterman said sharply. "Sit down, Nick." She wrote Italy on the board, then turned around.

"Minoru?"

The new student said in a clear voice. "My parents came to this country seventeen years ago. They were from Japan, but I am an American."

"Dirty Jap," Roy muttered.

This time Barb was on her feet with Nick, and they both went after Roy!

CHAPTER 10

Good-bye to a President

"Barbara Harrington, I'm surprised at you," Mrs. Counterman said. She had taken Barb, Nick, and Roy out into the hall after she gave the students a reading assignment.

"Me? What about the others?" Barb said, although she was a bit surprised at her own reaction to Roy's name calling. She had never hit anyone in her life, except Eddie, and that had been a long time ago. She hadn't actually hit Roy. Good sense had taken over once Mrs. Counterman had ordered them back to their desks. But Barb had wanted to hit him.

"You want to start World War III?" Mrs. Counterman asked instead of answering the question. "This assignment was to make things better, not worse. Nick, you must hold your temper. You two boys apologize to each other."

Nick looked at Roy and muttered "I'm sorry" in an insincere manner. Roy did the same.

"Go back into the room, Nick, and get out your reading book."

Nick walked back inside. Mrs. Counterman took Barb and Roy by the arms and walked them farther down the hall, out of earshot of the students in the classroom.

"Now, Roy, I want you to straighten up. What's your problem with Americans who have been here only one or two generations?"

"I don't have a problem," Roy said.

"I think I'll have a talk with your parents," Mrs. Counterman said.

"No," Roy said quickly. "They're real busy working for the war."

"I'll call them tonight," Mrs. Counterman said, "unless you want to tell me what it is that has you calling people names."

"Are you really English on both sides?" Barb asked.

"Yes," Roy said so defensively that Barb suspected that he wasn't. He had straight black hair and a round face, but that didn't tell her anything about his heritage.

"That's not the issue here," Mrs. Counterman said. "Barb, apologize to Roy. You, too," she ordered Roy.

"Sorry," Barb mumbled in a low voice at the same time that Roy muttered something she couldn't make out.

"You may go back in the room," Mrs. Counterman told Barb.

Before she slipped into the room, Barb glanced back and saw Mrs. Counterman wagging a finger at Roy. She hoped he got in deep trouble.

When Mrs. Counterman and Roy came back into the room, the social studies lesson continued. Students gave their information, and the teacher wrote it on the board.

"We have nineteen countries represented," Mrs. Counterman said. "Our textbook calls America a 'melting pot' of nationalities. Wouldn't you agree that that's true?"

The students nodded. Maybe the lesson had an effect on them, but Barb had thought there would be an instant opening of arms to the Japanese boys. There was not. Looking at ancestors had worked for Carolyn, but her family had been in the country the same length of time as Yoko's, just from a different country.

Barb held up her hand. The class seemed subdued, as if no one wanted to cause a stir because of the earlier outburst. Maybe she could lighten the moment.

"Yes, Barbara?"

"My Aunt Daisy, who's not my real aunt, but we call her that," she explained, "says her ancestors met the *Mayflower*."

Mrs. Counterman chuckled, just as Aunt Daisy did, but the rest of the class didn't. Maybe it was grown-up humor.

"What does she mean by that?" Mrs. Counterman asked the class.

A boy held up his hand, and the teacher nodded at him. "Indians were here first."

"Exactly. Barbara's Aunt Daisy must have some Indian blood." Mrs. Counterman cast a sidelong glance at Roy, and Barb figured that he was part Indian and didn't want to say it. That fit with his straight hair, but his skin wasn't red. And what was wrong with admitting that he was part Indian if he was?

"Who exactly is an American?" Mrs. Counterman said. No one answered. "Would all American citizens please stand up."

The entire class stood.

"So we're all Americans," she said. "Someday you will all have the right to vote in our democracy. Does your vote count more if your family has lived here longer?"

"No," Nick said before a chorus of other voices answered the same thing.

"Then it's our duty to be good citizens, which includes respecting other people's opinions." At this point she glanced at Barb, who looked down at her desk.

Her grand idea of making the Japanese be accepted hadn't really worked. Her classmates had been hammered with anti-Jap sentiments for too long. It would take more than one social studies lesson to undo that, especially when the war went on and on.

At least the class discussion persuaded Warren to accept Yoko or at least not to object to her when she was in a group with him. He went with Barb, Yoko, Carolyn, and Eddie that Saturday to see *Meet Me in St. Louis*.

Fighting in the Philippines was on the newsreel. Barb mentioned it to Alice when they got back to the hotel, and Alice burst into tears.

Barb hugged her. "The newsman said we were taking back ground."

"I know, but I'm so afraid they will find graves," Alice said. "I'm afraid Jim is dead."

Barb had known that all along, so she was surprised that Alice had just now come to that conclusion. "Aunt Daisy says we should face our fears." She went through Aunt Daisy's reasoning about the worst that could happen. "So we pray that God was with him," Barb said.

"Is with him," Alice said with a catch in her voice. "I'll pray that God is with him, that his time on earth isn't over, and that I'll see him again. You're a smart girl, Barb."

"Aunt Daisy's smart. She told me," Barb admitted, although she raised her chin just a little bit higher.

Soon the news was full of the Russians finding a concentration camp at Auschwitz. Thousands of Jews had been killed, and many were starving to death in the camp.

"What if Jim is in a horrible death camp like that?" Alice was beside herself again.

"You keep praying that God is with him," Barb said.

"Yes, you're right," Alice said and fingered the cross on the necklace that Jim had given her before he'd gone into the navy. "I tell Jim's mother that whenever she calls. I just need to remind myself."

The war droned on and on. Letters from Steve were further apart. He was in Belgium, and Barb figured it was just a matter of time before he'd be in Germany itself. She looked at the atlas whenever a new letter arrived, and she looked at the atlas when she heard a specific town mentioned on the news. Never before had she been aware of the countries of Europe. Now she thought she would never forget them.

She liked the newsreels. There she could see actual moving pictures of the war and of the leaders. In the newspaper, she saw President Roosevelt sitting with England's Churchill and Russia's Stalin when they met at Yalta, but on the newsreel it looked more real. Barb looked up Yalta in the atlas and had a hard time finding the Crimean port in the Black Sea.

"Why did they pick this place instead of somewhere in the United States?" Barb asked her dad. Yalta was in Asia, but wasn't there always a risk of a German airplane dropping a bomb anywhere over there?

"It's hard for us to understand everything about politics," Dad said. "They have more information than we do, and I'm sure President Roosevelt is doing the best he can to end this war."

During March the government asked the public not only to conserve paper, but to turn in all scrap paper to collection centers. A special appeal went to the Boy Scouts. The War Production Board would award the General Eisenhower Waste Paper Medal to any Boy Scout who collected at least a thousand pounds of waste paper during the March and April campaign.

"Why didn't they ask Girl Scouts?" Barb asked Eddie after he returned from his Scout meeting one afternoon.

He shrugged. "Don't ask me. I didn't do it. But since we can't have a race, why don't you girls help Warren and me collect paper?"

"Sure," Barb said, but she'd rather have had a project of her own. In the past, she might have objected to helping Eddie. But since he'd had polio, she looked at him differently. In an odd way, the disease had brought them closer together.

Barb, Carolyn, and Yoko banded together with Eddie and Warren to collect every scrap they could. Besides the collection site set up in the lobby where residents could put their old newspapers, the kids went door to door, much as they had for the grease drives to get fat for ammunition.

They walked up and down Yesler Way, asking the businesses there for waste paper. The cigar store had some stuff. Eddie and Warren went into the union office, where men hung around in front. They came back empty-handed, but told the girls what the dark, smoke-filled place was like inside.

Not to be outdone, Carolyn marched past the closed ticket booth and knocked on the door of the burlesque house, a place Barb had been forbidden to go near. Mama's exact words were, Don't go within ten feet of that place. Barb stood by the curb, as far away from the door as she could be and still see the action.

A quite ordinary-looking woman answered the door. Barb had expected a garish woman in an outlandish costume, but the woman seemed nice, and she brought back old programs and gave them to Carolyn.

"We're supposed to go by every week, and she'll have more," Carolyn said.

"Let's put them at the bottom of the pile," Barb suggested. No need in rousing Mama's curiosity over something that she hadn't done wrong. Barb hadn't gone within ten feet of the place. She'd probably been eleven feet away.

Their pile of papers grew. Eddie and Warren took them to the collection center and had them weighed and the poundage added to their accounts.

One April day as Barb and the others walked home from school, they talked about going back out after supper and collecting again. They were only a half block from the hotel when they met a young woman with tears streaming down her face.

Without a moment's hesitation, Barb stepped in front of the woman.

"What's wrong? Can we help you?" Barb asked.

The woman looked down at her and wiped her tears with a handkerchief. "The president is dead," she whispered with a sob.

"President Roosevelt?" Eddie said.

"Yes. What will the country do now? Who will lead us through this war?"

"President Roosevelt is dead?" Barb asked. Surely the woman was mistaken. Barb had seen pictures of him at that Yalta conference. "Did someone kill him?"

"No. The radio said he died of a cerebral hemorrhage."

"What?" Eddie asked.

"Like a stroke," the woman said and sniffed into her handkerchief.

"Let's go," Barb said. She didn't really believe this woman. She needed to hear it from the radio.

The friends ran to the hotel as fast as they could. The radio was on in the lobby and several residents, including Mr. Lazarini and Mrs. Hunter, were sitting around listening to it. Mrs. Wakamutsu sat in the office.

"Is it true?" Barb asked her.

"Yes," she replied.

Barb ran to the apartment, with the other kids on her heels. Mama, Alice, Audrey, Frank, and the Wakamutsu boys were crammed in the living room, some sitting, some standing. No one was talking except the announcer on the radio. Barb sat on the floor and listened.

While the message from the sponsor was on, Mama said, "He was in Warm Springs, Georgia, at the Little White House. That's the headquarters of the March of Dimes." She wiped away a tear.

"Who is Harry Truman?" Eddie asked.

"The vice president, of course," Audrey said. "Well, president now."

"What will happen?" Barb asked.

"Nothing different," Alice said. "I suspect President Truman will continue with President Roosevelt's policies. The war plan will go forward."

"I wonder how Mrs. Roosevelt is bearing up," Mama said.

The newscaster was back on and repeated the news he had already given. The group sat in silence once again, listening.

Barb didn't go out collecting papers. She sat glued to the

radio, listening, hoping the announcer would say there had been a bad mistake. She went to bed hoping to wake up the next day and learn this had all been a nightmare. She had liked the president. He'd had polio like Eddie, which made her feel a special bond with him.

The next morning the nightmare didn't go away. The newspaper headline screamed that President Roosevelt was dead. War news went on for pages. The American army had pushed beyond the Elbe River. At one point, only seventy-five miles separated the Russian and American troops, with Berlin in-between. Barb should have looked it up on the map, but she didn't feel like it. Another article said more than four hundred B-29 Superfortresses had bombed Tokyo for two hours. That plane had been designed at the Boeing plant. Barb should have felt proud, but all she felt was numb.

Barb couldn't shake this unsettled feeling. She wondered about the future of the country. How did President Truman feel now that he was the leader of the nation? Like she did sometimes when she was in charge of the class meetings and selling the war stamps?

"Face your fear," she said aloud. She prayed that God had been with President Roosevelt when he died and that he would be with President Truman now.

CHAPTER 11

The Balloon Bomb

Barb read everything she could about the new president. She and the other students in Mrs. Counterman's class listened to his speech to Congress the day after President Roosevelt had been laid to rest in New York.

"He's asked the country to help him and asked for God's help," Aunt Daisy told Barb after school. "Can't ask for more than that. Besides, he's from Missouri, right next door to Oklahoma. That means he's got common sense."

Later on the newsreel at the movie, Barb, Yoko, and Carolyn saw Harry Truman being sworn in as president. The newsreel was also full of pictures from the death camps in Germany. The pictures of half-starved people in Buchenwald and Belsen made Barb sick.

Carolyn leaned over Barb and whispered to Yoko, "It wasn't like that in the camp you went to, was it?"

"Oh, no. We were in small quarters, and the food was not very good, but it was nothing like that."

"I'm glad German descendants weren't sent to camps," Carolyn said.

Barb was, too.

"My relatives didn't do this to those people," Carolyn said and motioned to the screen where pictures of the concentration camps still flickered.

"Or mine," Barb said.

"And mine didn't bomb Pearl Harbor," Yoko said.

What a mixed-up time, Barb thought. *Countries do horrible things to each other, yet ordinary people wouldn't do such bad things.*

Mrs. Counterman had the students bring in newspaper clippings about the United Nations conference that started the end of April in San Francisco. They talked about how many nations would likely join and how this would be a way to keep the world at peace.

"The United Nations might be a 'melting pot,' just like the United States," Mrs. Counterman said, and Barb hoped that would be true.

Troops were closing in on Berlin, but the war effort on the home front continued as the paper drive came to a close.

Eddie and Warren and the girls carried a load of scrap paper to the collection center on Saturday after they finished morning chores. They'd been carrying paper forever, it seemed. And every time they went to the center, Eddie's and Warren's accounts went up fifteen or twenty pounds.

"What does this make it?" Eddie asked after the paper was weighed in.

"Almost there. Just another twenty-two pounds," the collection worker said.

Warren's load was weighed in and came to twenty-four pounds. He still needed eighteen more.

"Monday's the end of the month, boys. This place will be a madhouse then. If you can, bring more paper this afternoon."

"We've already been to all our collection sites. Where else can we go?" Barb asked as they made their way to the hotel.

"We haven't been back to the burlesque house," Carolyn said. She'd told her mom about that collection place and been forbidden to return. "That woman probably has tons of old programs for us."

"But we can't go there again," Eddie said. "None of us is allowed to go near that place."

"I have an idea," Barb said. "Maybe under the circumstances my mother and Mrs. Wakamutsu would give us one-time permission to go there, just to get the paper. It is for the war, after all."

"What do we have to lose?" Warren asked, and the group raced off to the Fairfax.

To their relief, both Mama and Mrs. Wakamutsu were home. As soon as Eddie explained the problem, the two women looked at each other. Barb held her breath.

"Because this is for the war," Mama said slowly, "you may go this one time."

Barb started breathing again.

"But," Mama continued, "it is not a good place for you to

be, and you are not to go near there again. Is that understood?"

Barb and Eddie nodded.

"Yoko," Mrs. Wakamutsu said, "you may also go. It will be a way to help your father win the war. But be careful."

The five friends walked briskly toward the hotel, but when they approached the burlesque house, they slowed their pace and looked nervously at each other.

"Who's going to knock on the door?" Warren asked. No one answered.

"I will go ask," Yoko finally said. She walked to the door and knocked softly.

A man answered. "What do you want, little Jap?"he barked.

Yoko stepped back.

"Scrap paper collection for the Boy Scouts."

"You don't look like no Boy Scout." He looked at Barb and the others. "You with them?"

"I'm collecting for my father, who is a soldier."

"I'll bet. For the emperor!" he said and slammed the door.

Barb marched to the door and pounded on it.

"Hey, mister," she called.

The man opened the door. "I thought—What's this?"

"My friend's dad is in the United States Army in Europe. Now do you have any scrap paper for the drive? Any old programs?"

"What is it?" a voice called from behind the man. The woman Barb had seen before came to the door. This time she wore heavy makeup and a glittery dress. She looked at the kids, and Barb saw recognition in her eyes when she spotted Carolyn. "Oh, I wondered when you'd come back for the papers. They've been piling up. Hurry up, kids. In a few minutes we'll be opening the ticket booth for the afternoon show. I want you out of here before then."

Barb led the way and motioned for the others to follow. She strained to look around, but they were led down a closed hallway, so she couldn't even see the stage.

There had to be a ton of paper in the huge pile in the back room. The five friends loaded up until they could carry no more and trudged to the front door. Before they left, Barb turned to the woman. "Yoko's father is fighting in the 442nd. He's a war hero. Tell that man."

"I'll tell him, honey, but I doubt it does much good."

"Thank you for the papers," Eddie said as they filed out of the burlesque house and headed to the collection center.

Barb walked alongside Yoko. "Sorry about that man."

"It is not your fault," Yoko said and shrugged. "I am used to it."

The kids struggled along under their loads in silence, an oddity for them.

"We're back," Eddie said fifteen minutes later when they dumped their loads on the scales.

The man looked at the programs, then said, "I guess paper's paper no matter where you got it."

Between the five of them, they had fifty-seven pounds. The man divided the number between Warren's and Eddie's accounts and proclaimed them both winners of the Eisenhower medal.

"Wow!" Eddie exclaimed. "When do we get it?"

"Your troop leader will award it," the man said.

The kids walked with light steps back toward the hotel. As they neared the burlesque house again, Warren said, "It took guts to knock on that door, Yoko. You earned part of the medal."

"I will take a corner piece," she said.

"What?" Warren said.

Yoko giggled, the first time Barb had ever heard her laugh. "It is a joke," she said.

"I'll let you wear it sometime," Warren said, and Barb vowed silently to hold him to that promise.

During the following week, tension mounted in the hotel as news from the European front gave hope that the end of the war was likely to occur at any moment. With the news of Hitler's suicide, Barb rejoiced. Surely that meant that the war couldn't go on any longer. But the Germans held out for another week. Finally the official announcement came from President Truman. The Germans had unconditionally surrendered.

Barb's first reaction was that Steve would be coming home, safe and sound. Yoko's father would come home, too.

But President Truman's V-E Day broadcast that she heard before she went to school and again in Mrs. Counterman's room made her rethink the situation. "Our victory is but half-won," the president said. "The West is free, but the East is still in bondage to the treacherous tyranny of the Japanese. When the last Japanese division has surrendered unconditionally, then only will our fighting job be done."

Mrs. Counterman made the issue crystal clear when she followed the announcement of the victory in Europe with a secret warning to the students.

"I'm going to tell you a story, and I want you to take it to heart. It's very important that you know this, but in a way it's a secret," she began.

"Last Saturday the Reverend Archie Mitchell, his wife, and four boys and a girl from their church went on a picnic in the south part of Oregon. It's unclear exactly what happened. Reverend Mitchell was parking the car when his wife called out for him to come see what they had found. There was a loud explosion, and Reverend Mitchell found the five children dead and his wife barely alive and her clothes on fire. He burned his hands trying to put out the flames, but his wife died within minutes. The children had found a Japanese balloon that held bombs."

Gasps echoed around the room, and Barb looked at the wide-eyed stares of the other students.

"I suspect that someone touched the balloon and it exploded," Mrs. Counterman said. "It made a hole three feet across, and there was shrapnel everywhere. If any of you see such a balloon, you are to run away from it and report it immediately to the police."

"How many are there?" Barb asked.

"I don't know."

"Where are they coming from?" Roy Madison asked.

"The authorities are unsure. It could be that a Japanese ship has released them, or it could be that they have been released from Japan. Perhaps there are no more of them, but the government doesn't want the Japanese to know that any balloons have landed here.

"That's where the secret comes in. The government wants no mention of this on the radio or in the newspapers. If the Japanese find out they have been successful, they may send more balloon bombs. But be sure to tell your parents and your brothers and sisters and others that you trust. They should be warned."

"What do the balloons look like?" a student asked.

"I haven't seen one, but the principal told us they were made of layers of paper and string. The balloon part is thirty feet across, and the bombs are hung below it. They are normally pearl-gray in color. Don't touch them! Remember, there will be no reports of this in the newspapers or on the radio. We don't want the Japanese to know the balloons are reaching us.

"What's the motto? Loose lips. . ." Mrs. Counterman started.

"Sink ships," the class said in unison.

"Three of the children killed were thirteen. One boy was

fourteen, and one was your age, eleven. Be careful and be watchful, boys and girls. I don't want to lose any of you. Now, you can go out for recess a little early."

The students filed silently out of the room and headed for the playground. There was no laughing and poking each other, like the boys normally did when they went outside.

As soon as the other classes had recess, Barb and Warren found the others. "Did your teacher tell you about the balloon bomb?" she asked.

"One boy was our age," Eddie said quietly.

That night Barb told both families about the balloons.

"President Truman is right," Dad said. "We have reason to celebrate tonight, but the war is only half-won. I wonder if Steve will be sent to the Pacific."

Barb hadn't thought of that possibility. Now she murmured, "God be with him."

CHAPTER 12

Good-bye, Hotel

"I'm worried about Raymond," Aunt Daisy confessed to Barb one afternoon while she was working in the office alone. Eddie and Warren were at Boy Scouts, and Mama and Mrs. Wakamutsu were cleaning out another empty room for some repair work.

"Why?"

"It's been over a month since I heard from him. I'm afraid he's been sent to Okinawa."

Barb got out the atlas, and they looked at the distance from Guam to the bigger island. The United States had already taken

Iwo Jima from the Japanese, and the newsreel showed it had taken heavy fighting to win. Japanese soldiers hid artillery guns in caves and rained bullets on Americans. Radio reports from the Pacific talked about hand-to-hand combat.

"There isn't an American airfield on Okinawa yet, is there?" Barb asked. Since they'd learned from the code that Raymond worked keeping planes flying, it made sense that he would be at an airfield. "Maybe he's been sent to Iwo Jima."

"Maybe."

"Face your fear," Barb reminded her.

"I know, but the Japanese fight until they're killed. And I don't know what to think of the kamikaze pilots. Those men know they're going to die before they climb in their airplanes."

"They must be crazy," Barb said. She'd seen a picture in the newspaper of a wrecked kamikaze plane burning on the deck of an American ship. She and Carolyn had talked about how insane those Japanese were to ram their planes into ships in the hopes of sinking them. They had been careful not to talk about it in front of Yoko. Her entire heritage was from Japan, and she observed some of their customs. Barb didn't feel comfortable talking about the Pacific war in front of her.

"You know what I think, Barb," Aunt Daisy said in a low voice. "I've started looking at each one of these men as someone's son. For every one killed, there's a mother out there who will never be the same."

"But we're at war," Barb said. "It's our country against their country. If we don't kill them, they'll kill us."

"I know, but that doesn't make it right," Aunt Daisy said.

"Mail here?" Mrs. Hunter called from a little ways down the hall.

"Yes, ma'am," Barb said. "You have a letter."

Mrs. Hunter didn't get a lot of mail, and what she got was usually postmarked from Atlanta. Barb handed over the letter and the afternoon newspaper. Then she turned her attention back to the map.

"American troops are getting closer and closer to Japan," Aunt Daisy said. "It's just a matter of time before they invade, but if the little islands have caused such fierce fighting, I can't imagine what the soldiers will face on Japan."

"Nooohh!"

Barb looked at the couch when she heard the groan of anguish. The letter fluttered to Mrs. Hunter's lap. Tears streamed down her face.

"Mrs. Hunter!" Aunt Daisy reached her first. "What is it?"

Mrs. Hunter motioned to the letter, and Aunt Daisy picked it up and quickly scanned it.

"Is this your sister's boy?"

Mrs. Hunter nodded.

"Barb, get your mother."

With wings on her feet, Barb ran to the room where Mama and Mrs. Wakamutsu were working. "Hurry, it's Mrs. Hunter," Barb said and fled back to the lobby. Barb felt helpless, just as she had when Mr. Wiley's Tommy had been killed. The end of the war seemed near with victory in sight, but still men were dying.

Mama, Mrs. Wakamutsu, and Aunt Daisy took Mrs. Hunter back to her apartment. Mrs. Wakamutsu came to the office and told Barb that Mrs. Hunter's nephew was missing in action on Okinawa. To Barb that meant he was dead, just like she knew Jim Watson was dead.

Supper was a quiet affair with the news of Mrs. Hunter's nephew hanging over the two families. Mama had helped her call her sister from the office and later had taken a tray of food to her apartment.

"Will she go to her sister's?" Eddie asked.

"No. She'll stay here and wait for news," Mama said.

"She could have a long wait," Alice said quietly. Barb looked at her sister, who had tears welling in her eyes.

When would it all be over? When would they know the truth about Jim? Someone at school had told her it was seven years after a war before a missing-in-action person could be declared dead. Alice was twenty-four now. In seven years she'd be thirty-one, an old maid. Barb doubted she would go out with any man on a date during that seven years. She sure hadn't gone out since Jim had been sent to the Philippines.

Dad called a two-family meeting in the living room after supper dishes were done, since they couldn't all sit at the kitchen table during the meal.

He started with a prayer for Mrs. Hunter and her nephew and, of course, remembered Steve, Jim, Raymond, Harry Muraro, and all the soldiers fighting the war.

"I've talked to our renters, and they assured me that their families will be out of our house by the first of June. School's out next week, so you kids will have time to help your mother pack our belongings, and we'll be moving on Saturday, June 2. I arranged for a truck today."

"We're going home?" Eddie asked.

"It'll be different living back there," Barb said. There had been many times that she'd wanted to go back to a time before the war, but now she could hardly remember a time when she didn't live at the hotel. She struggled with memories and associated the two-story house on Queen Anne Hill with homemade ice cream and cookies. It was the sugar house. There had been no sugar rationing before the war, so she had taken desserts for granted.

"We are in your debt for keeping the Fairfax running during our time at the camp," Mr. Wakamutsu said. "We would have nothing now if you had not been such good friends."

Barb would be out of a job. Her time in the office would be over. What would they do during the summer in their own house? There would be no hallways to scrub and no linens to change. No bustle of people on the street below. No Aunt Daisy to talk to. No Carolyn. No Yoko. No Mrs. Hunter.

She could hardly stand it until the meeting was over. As soon as Dad had finished answering questions, she scurried out the door and down to Aunt Daisy's apartment.

"What's wrong?" Aunt Daisy said the minute she opened the door.

"We're moving!" Barb wailed and rushed inside.

"I figured you'd be going soon, with school getting out and all. It'll be nice for your folks to be back in their own home."

"But when will I see you?" Barb asked, following Aunt Daisy to the tiny kitchen. "And what about Carolyn?"

"I can't answer about Carolyn, but you'll see me." Aunt Daisy got out two glasses and the ice trays. "I have Raymond's car, you know, and I can drive anywhere I want. Electric buses run from near your house to the corner, so you could come here for next to nothing."

She poured iced tea and handed a glass to Barb, who took a big gulp. It was unsweetened, of course. After the war Barb could go back to drinking sweetened tea. The sugar house. That's where she was going. There had to be good things about it.

There was the big room she shared with Audrey. It was twice the size of the room the two of them shared with Yoko.

117

"Things will be different," Aunt Daisy said. "But change is usually good. Look at how you've changed since you moved here."

"How?" Barb asked. She hadn't noticed change. She'd always been the same Barb.

"You and Eddie have become friends instead of being so competitive. And you've been very responsible in the office. You should work for the post office when you get older."

"I want to be a politician," Barb said and was surprised that she'd said that. She hadn't given her future any real thought, but she liked being in charge of things.

Aunt Daisy nodded. "I believe there will be a time when women will be candidates for the House of Representatives and the Senate. Why, look how Frances Perkins was on President Roosevelt's cabinet all these years. It's just a matter of time until women will be elected."

"Maybe there'll be a woman governor," Barb said.

"Could be. Anything's possible. But you didn't have any idea of running for class president before you moved here. See how you've changed? And you'll keep changing."

"Until I'm grown up."

"No, you'll keep changing even after that."

Barb finished her tea and walked down the hall, her head spinning with thoughts of the future. Eddie intercepted her in the lobby.

"What do you think about moving?" he asked.

"It'll be a big change, and there'll be a lot of things I'll miss, but there will be some good things, too."

"Like what?" he asked and fell in step with her as they headed to the apartment.

"My room has that big window. I used to love looking out at

the backyard and that big tree where Frank had that tree house."

"Hey, we'll have a yard again," Eddie said. "I might talk Mama into letting me have a dog. I wonder if Warren. . ." He trailed off.

"Electric buses run from here to there," Barb said. "He can ride out and play with your dog."

"And we could come downtown some days."

"Sure. See, there are good things," Barb said as she opened the door to the apartment.

The next day at school she repeated that same phrase as she told Carolyn about the move. She'd given it a lot of thought and had several options, she called them, a word she'd seen politicians use in the paper.

They could form a club, and on Tuesdays Carolyn and Yoko could ride out to Queen Anne Hill, and on Fridays she could come downtown. Or on Mondays she could come to town, and on Thursdays they could come to her house.

"Or we could meet halfway and have lunch," Carolyn said with a high-society accent.

Barb laughed. This might work. She'd be in a new school next year, but she'd have to make the most of it. Probably as the new girl, she wouldn't be elected class president, but she wouldn't worry about that. Right now she had the last-day-of-school picnic to plan and money to collect for the gift the class would give to Mrs. Counterman.

The picnic went off well, with races, tug-of-war, and other games. It was almost time for the class to go inside to get their report cards. That was when they'd give the teacher the gift. Barb was standing by the outside door when Roy Madison walked by.

"Roy, can I talk to you a minute?" He stopped and eyed her suspiciously. "Are you part Indian?" she asked. Barb figured she'd never see him again after this day anyway, but she had wondered since that time she'd almost hit him for making bad comments about other people's ancestors.

He stared at her with dark eyes for a long moment, and she didn't think he would answer her question. "I'm part Eskimo," he finally said. "So what?"

Barb shrugged. "I think that's neat. Why'd you hide it?"

Now he shrugged. "I don't know. But I'm part English, too."

"We're both Americans," Barb said. "It doesn't matter where we came from."

"Maybe," he said.

"Do you want to present the gift to Mrs. Counterman?" she asked impulsively as a gesture of peace.

"Okay. Sure, I'll do it."

Barb called the last class meeting to order when everyone was in from the playground. She gave a report on how many war stamps they had bought during the year, the highest in the school. Then she called Roy to the front to make the teacher presentation.

Mrs. Counterman looked stunned as she opened the gift, a card that all the students had signed and some hard-to-get perfume. "This is heavenly," she said. "Such a nice fragrance. Thank you all so much. This is a class I will never forget."

One by one, Mrs. Counterman called her students to the front to receive their report cards. Then the final bell of the year rang, and the class was dismissed. Everyone rushed to the door with shouts of joy about summer vacation.

"Barbara Harrington, could I see you a moment?" Mrs. Counterman asked before Barb could leave.

"Yes, ma'am." Barb couldn't imagine what her teacher wanted. She hadn't done anything wrong at the meeting.

The teacher waited until the other students had left, then she turned to Barb. "It's been a real pleasure having you as the class president. You're a smart girl. I've known that all along, but today you showed one more sign of it. You read people very well. You can see when they're hurt and when they need help. Now tell me, why did you let Roy give me the perfume?"

"I don't know. I guess it was my way of saying I was sorry for the way I almost attacked him that one day. I'll never see him again, since we're moving next weekend, but I didn't want to leave it bad between us."

Mrs. Counterman hugged her. "You're going to go very far in life. Make all good choices, Barbara."

"Think I can be governor some day?" Barb asked with a grin.

"I don't know why not. Be sure and ask your old teacher to your inauguration."

The others were waiting to walk home, but Barb couldn't share her teacher's good-bye with them. It was personal and would sound like bragging. There was a time when that wouldn't have stopped her, but Aunt Daisy was right. She had changed.

CHAPTER 13

The End of the War

The week between school being out and the family's move back to Queen Anne Hill was filled to the brim with work, packing, and saying good-bye.

Aunt Daisy had a good-bye party for them in the lobby on Friday night. It reminded Barb of the Christmas Eve party when Mr. Wiley had been there.

Since Yoko had grown attached to Mittens, and it had been the Wakamutsus' cat originally, Isabel gave it to Yoko at the party.

"Mittens's home is at the hotel," Isabel said. "It wouldn't be right to make her leave."

"You are very kind," Yoko said. She held the cat close to her heart.

Kaneko presented a pen and ink drawing of the hotel to the Harringtons. "So you will remember your time here," he said.

Barb knew that she would never forget it.

On Saturday, Mr. Wakamutsu drove to the front of the hotel in the borrowed truck. Frank, Kaneko, and Abiko carried the little furniture the family had brought with them down the stairs. Warren and Carolyn came over to carry boxes, and Audrey, Alice, Barb, Yoko, Mrs. Wakamutsu, Mama, and Aunt Daisy struggled with household goods and boxes of clothes.

Sitting in the office chair was none other than Mrs. Hunter. Barb had suggested to Mrs. Wakamutsu that Mrs. Hunter could watch the office while the others helped with the move. Barb had remembered how Mrs. Hunter had liked it when she'd done that one other time, and right now Mrs. Hunter needed something to take her mind off her nephew's MIA status.

Barb was feeling pretty smug. If there was one thing she had learned recently, it was that turning old enemies into friends was a way of helping herself feel good. Not that Mrs. Hunter or Roy Madison were enemies, but there had been friction between Barb and them in the past. Now that was eased.

Mama, the older girls, and Aunt Daisy had spent Friday at

the house getting it cleaned and ready. As soon as the truck was loaded, the moving crew piled in it or in Aunt Daisy's car to drive to the house. A good deal of the family's belongings, chest of drawers, beds, even the kitchen table, had been stored in the attic. Now the boys wrestled them down the steep stairs and into the rooms Mama pointed out.

Barb thought her bed making was over with the move from the hotel, but she and Carolyn were put on bed-making detail.

"First thing is to make the beds," Mama said. "Then when we're too tired to unpack one more box, we can fall into bed."

Barb and Carolyn went from room to room, carrying clean linens.

"This is a great house," Carolyn said once they were in Barb's room.

"I know. Especially this room. I used to stand here and look down at the backyard. That tree has really grown since we've been gone. I helped Dad plant that one over there when we moved in. I'll bet it's taller than Dad."

The place buzzed with activity. Aunt Daisy and Mama worked in the kitchen. Mrs. Wakamutsu helped the girls hang clothes in the built-in closets, and the boys toted box after box from the truck.

"Dad and Isabel will be shocked when they see this," Barb said. The living room looked homey with the old familiar couch and chairs facing the fireplace.

At noon, the Wakamutsus departed to return the truck and get back to their work at the hotel. Aunt Daisy took Mama to the grocery store, and after the food was unloaded, she left, giving Carolyn and Warren a ride home.

"Well, kids, it's just us," Mama said, looking around her

with obvious pleasure. "Seems quiet, doesn't it?"

It almost seemed lonely to Barb, but she still had tons to do, so she worked in her room, getting her things arranged. The smell of baking chocolate drew her to the kitchen.

"What is that?" she asked.

"Chocolate cake. Daisy's been saving the chocolate, and I spent my ration on sugar for our first night back home." Mama said it with such pleasure, that Barb realized the years they had spent at the hotel had been a real sacrifice for her. But she'd run the hotel in the name of friendship, and Barb doubted that Mama regretted it.

Although there were no pictures on the walls or knickknacks out on the small lamp tables in the living room, the house looked like a home by the time Dad and Isabel returned from work. Dinner was a festive occasion, and the chocolate cake was cause in itself for celebration.

That night as she lay in bed in the familiar, yet strange room, Barb wondered what was going on at the hotel, but she was glad to be back at the sugar house.

On Sunday after Dad and Isabel had gone off to work, Barb and the others rode the electric bus downtown to church and then returned to the house. Never had a Sunday afternoon dragged out so long. Before, when they'd lived in the house, Sunday afternoons had been family times. But now they weren't a whole family. Dad and Isabel were working, and Steve was gone.

By late Monday morning, everything was in its place in the house, and Barb was at a loss for what to do. Eddie had worked on Frank's old bicycle, but it needed a new tire, and there weren't any available. Audrey's bike was in just as bad shape. When the war was over, he could fix them both up, and maybe he and Barb could ride around in the neighborhood.

Mama called on the neighbors to tell them they were back, and Barb and Eddie walked around the area, becoming familiar again with old places. Eddie's limp seemed more pronounced. Barb wondered if his weakened leg bothered him more in the summer than in the winter, but she didn't ask. She didn't want him to know that she'd noticed.

They talked about the different people who lived in the neighborhood as they passed house after house, and their steps led them to the school. The playground was smaller than Barb remembered, but still larger than the one at the school downtown.

"Remember Mrs. Dean?" Eddie asked. "I wonder if she still teaches first grade."

"She was nice," Barb said. "I wonder if Helen Ishmael still goes to school here." She wouldn't be exactly the new girl in school if she was in the same classroom as some of the kids she remembered. She'd have to reacquaint herself with them, that was all. Maybe she wouldn't be elected class president, but she might be vice president. That hope made her step a little lighter.

They walked home and found only Frank and Audrey there. "Mama and Alice took the bus downtown after Aunt Daisy called. Mrs. Hunter was notified that her nephew was killed in action."

"Does that mean they found his body?" Eddie asked.

"I guess it does. Mama said they might not have been able to identify it before," Audrey said.

Barb wanted to go to the hotel, but she obeyed Mama's orders to stay home and help with the yard work. After all, she was going downtown tomorrow to meet Carolyn and Yoko for their first friendship club meeting. Eddie was going, too, since Mama thought the twins ought to ride the bus together.

Frank pushed the mower, and the twins picked up fallen sticks and pulled weeds out of what had been a flower garden when they had lived there three years earlier, but had been turned into a Victory garden with tomato plants and onion sets.

"We had lots healthier plants in our Victory garden," Eddie said. "They probably didn't use the right fertilizer or talk to the plants."

"They're still little," Barb said. "By the end of summer we could have juicy tomatoes."

They finished the work and waited on the small porch for Mama to return. When she came home, she reported that Mrs. Hunter was doing as well as could be expected.

Barb picked a small bouquet of roses from the climbing bush in the backyard and took them to Mrs. Hunter the next afternoon when she and Eddie rode the bus downtown. The girls traded news of what they'd been doing, and Barb was a little annoyed that Carolyn was continuing last summer's habit of visiting the hotel each afternoon. She felt left out but tried to push that feeling down.

Barb visited with Aunt Daisy a few minutes before time for her to meet Eddie at the bus stop and go back home. She also picked up a letter from Steve that had been delivered to the hotel.

The summer fell into a pattern. Carolyn and Yoko came out to Queen Anne Hill on Friday afternoons, and Barb introduced them to some new friends in the neighborhood. Steve's letters started coming to the house, and although the war news continued to dominate the newspaper, Barb didn't keep up with it as she had when they'd lived in the hotel.

She seemed more removed from it now that school was out and they lived in a house again. There still wasn't much sugar, Mama continued to ride the bus down to the ration board, and Alice and Audrey continued their volunteer work with the Red Cross, but Barb knew it was just a matter of time now until the war with Japan would be over.

She read of President Truman going to the Potsdam Conference the end of July and saw his picture in the paper with the Russian and English leaders. Out of habit, she got the atlas out of the bookshelf and found Potsdam right outside of Berlin.

Then the unimaginable occurred. Shortly after eight one August morning, Dad called home from the Boeing plant. He rarely called, so Barb knew something important had happened. Mama turned white and motioned for Eddie to turn on the radio. The newscaster was repeating a special war bulletin from the president.

"Sixteen hours ago an American airplane dropped one bomb on Hiroshima. . . . It is an atomic bomb. It is a harnessing of the basic power of the universe. . . ."

"What does that mean?" Audrey asked.

Barb had no idea. She listened to a vague explanation by the newscaster about destroying Japanese docks, factories, and their power to make war.

"It is a most terrible bomb." Mama wrung her hands as she talked. "Dad said it destroyed the entire city."

"Could that happen here?" Barb asked. She had no idea how many balloon bombs had been sent or if any more had landed. No one talked about them.

"I don't think Japan has the atomic bomb, but this is the place they would drop it if they did. They'd want to destroy the

Boeing plant. Dad said it was one of Boeing's B-29s that dropped the bomb."

"Does that mean the end of the war?" Frank asked. "If it destroyed Japan's factories, they can't make airplanes."

"I don't know," Mama said. "I imagine the end of the war is closer. Maybe Steve will be coming home soon." She reached for the telephone and called the hotel.

Barb heard her talking to Mrs. Wakamutsu.

"What did she say?" Barb asked once Mama had hung up the receiver.

"She's all right about it. Her sister lives in Tokyo, and Yoko's relatives live in Nagasaki."

Barb breathed a sigh of relief. At least her friends were not directly affected by the bombing.

But a few days later, the newspaper headline screamed about another bombing. This time Nagasaki was hit. Barb and Eddie took the bus into the hotel even though it was Thursday and the girls would be coming to their house the next day.

"How are you?" Barb asked Yoko.

"I am okay," she said, but she had tears in her eyes. "I don't know if my relatives were killed or injured. I never met them, but my father did. He is still in Germany. I received a letter from him yesterday. I know he must be grieving for his family."

"The Japanese have to surrender now," Eddie said, "or we'll keep bombing their cities. They have to give up. Then your father will come home."

The papers were full of the peace talks. American soldiers stopped bombing while the Allies considered Japan's surrender terms. At the same time, Russian troops invaded Manchuria in Asia, and news reached Seattle about the sinking of the *Indianapolis*, which was torpedoed by a Japanese submarine at the end of July. The ship had sunk in minutes, leaving many sailors adrift in the shark-infested waters for days before rescue ships had arrived. Many sailors had been eaten alive by the sharks.

Barb could hardly imagine such horror. With peace so close, men were still losing their lives in such hideous ways.

Days passed, and Barb and the others held their breaths, waiting.

On Tuesday afternoon, Carolyn, Warren, and Yoko were walking Barb and Eddie to the bus stop when a yell like Barb had never heard before came out of the labor union office, and men rushed out of the building.

"It's over!" One man's voice could be heard above the cheers.

"Japan surrendered!" another yelled.

Barb screamed. Tears of joy flooded her eyes.

The kids ran back up the sidewalk to the hotel and found people pouring onto the street from every building and business. Church bells rang. Factory whistles shrilled an end to the war. Firecrackers exploded in the alley. Women cried, and old men whooped. Children shouted and danced around on the sidewalk, twirling until they were so dizzy they fell down. The place was in chaos, and it didn't let up. It just got wilder.

Barb tried to call home from the office phone, but she couldn't get through. The lines were jammed.

"Stay here," Aunt Daisy said. "Your folks will know where you are."

Barb couldn't stay in the hotel when there was such excitement outside and the crowd was growing bigger and bigger. She rushed down the stairs and out on the sidewalk with the others.

From above it rained feathers like confetti. Barb looked up

in time to see Mrs. Hunter shaking a pillow's contents on the joyous crowd below.

"It's over!" Barb shouted. "It's over!"

CHAPTER 14

The Homecoming

Mama, Alice, Frank, and Audrey arrived at the hotel on the bus.

"What a wild ride," Frank told Barb and the others. "Everyone was crying and shouting and carrying on. It was great!"

Dad and Isabel went home after their work shift, read Mama's note, and wound up at the hotel, too. What a party! What a celebration!

"Raymond is coming home!" Aunt Daisy shouted, hugging everyone in sight. "My son made it through the war."

"Mine, too," Mama said. "I don't think he ever got shifted to the Pacific. But we'll find out soon."

Mrs. Wakamutsu smiled but was rather quiet compared to the others. Barb cornered Yoko and asked her about her foster mother.

"She told me," Yoko said, "that there is a line that cuts her in two. She loves America. It has been so good to her, and her children are American. Japan is home. She feels sorrow for her homeland, but she has no wish to ever return there."

"What about Mr. Wakamutsu?" Barb didn't know him nearly as well as she knew his wife.

"Long ago in the camp he told me that he felt like a child whose parents were arguing. He didn't care who won as long as the fighting stopped."

"Well, I'm glad it's over," Barb said.

"Me, too," Yoko said. "I am a loyal American. I want you to know that is true."

"I know that," Barb said.

Barb's family left the hotel after midnight. The next morning, although Dad and Isabel went to work as normal, the rest of the household dragged around, tired but happy.

"When will Steve get to come home?" Barb asked.

"I don't know," Mama said. "Dad says the army takes awhile to discharge soldiers, and some will be kept overseas to enforce the peace. We've waited this long, I suppose we can wait as long as it takes, now that we know he's coming home."

Exactly a week later, the phone rang. Barb picked it up, expecting Carolyn to be on the other line, but instead a woman's choked-up voice asked for Alice.

Barb covered the receiver with her hand. "Mama, it's for Alice," she whispered. "It sounds like a woman crying. I think it's Mrs. Watson." This was the call that Barb had dreaded for so long.

"Oh, no," Mama said. "I'll get her."

A moment later Alice walked into the living room with Mama on her heels. Alice took the phone and said timidly, "Hello?"

She listened for a second, then sank slowly to the floor. She said something that Barb couldn't make out because of her sobs. Tears poured down her cheeks, and her breath came in giant gasps. Finally Barb could understand. "Thank You, God. Thank You, God," Alice said over and over.

"Is he alive?" Mama asked.

Alice nodded, and still more tears came. Barb plopped on the floor and hugged her sister.

Mama took the phone. "Mrs. Watson? Mrs. Watson? Jim's all right?" She looked at Barb and nodded up and down.

Barb wiped her own tears. "Where is he?" she asked, but Alice could only shake her head.

"Eddie!" Barb yelled toward the stairs. "Eddie!"

He ran down the stairs, and his mouth flew open. "Frank!" he turned and yelled. "Come here."

"Jim's alive," Barb said and found she was having difficulty speaking, too. Both boys came in the living room and hugged Alice.

Mama hung up the phone and joined the group on the floor. "He was in a prison camp in Manchuria. He's in a hospital in China now."

"Hos. . .pi. . .tal?" Alice had the hiccups now.

"He's very weak. Prisoners weren't fed very well, but he's going to be all right," Mama said. "He'll be flown to a stateside hospital."

"Thank. . .God," Alice said.

"Yes, let's thank God right now," Mama said and led her children in prayer.

Audrey came home from a friend's house, and the tears of joy started again as the story was retold. Mama called Dad and the hotel, and Barb called her friends, and the news spread.

Barb still couldn't believe it. As more details were known, she was amazed that Jim had survived. A few days later, he cabled his parents and Alice and wrote that he'd made it through the Bataan Death March and then was taken to Manchuria from the Philippines, but now he was all right and would be coming home soon.

The days dragged by as August turned into September and the family waited. A triumphant letter arrived from Steve. When the news of the atomic bombs had reached his unit in Germany, the troops had celebrated. Their orders for the Pacific were canceled, and Steve knew he'd be coming home soon.

School started, which helped the wait go faster. Barb and Eddie were in the same classroom, which dismayed Barb. Wouldn't Eddie want to run for class president or vice president just as she wanted to? And could she run against him?

She didn't have to decide. This school didn't have class presidents. Disappointed, she settled down to regular school work and looked forward to Saturdays, when she could ride the bus downtown to the movies or to the hotel and watch all the action on the street. Servicemen returned to Seattle every day, and many drifted to the union office near the hotel.

The newsreel showed the surrender of the Japanese on the USS *Missouri* that was anchored in Tokyo Bay. Barb stayed after the feature movie to watch it again. The Japanese officials wore top hats and tails, as if they were dressed for a fancy ball.

They were giving up in style. That fit with the way the Waka-mutsus acted and even Yoko. They had grace and manners that had to have come from their Japanese heritage.

The last Saturday of September, Barb and Eddie made their usual trip downtown. As they walked from the bus stop to the hotel, Barb saw Aunt Daisy's car pull out from the curb and head their way.

Aunt Daisy was nowhere in sight. "Somebody's stealing her car," Barb shouted. She waved her arms at the car, and the man driving pulled over.

"Something wrong?" he called out the window.

The face was oddly familiar, although she didn't know the man.

"Raymond?" Eddie asked, and Barb knew immediately that he was right.

"Yes. Do I know you?" Raymond asked.

Barb introduced them, and he explained that he'd returned the night before. "Mama's up in the apartment. We stayed up nearly all night talking, so she's slow getting around this morning."

They stepped back so he could move on, and then they rushed up to Aunt Daisy's apartment to hear all about Raymond's return.

The second week in October, Eddie and Barb were walking home from school when three soldiers got off the bus at the corner ahead of them.

"There are more soldiers around here than you can shake a stick at," Eddie said.

The men had slung huge duffel bags over their shoulders. One man pointed toward their street, and the men turned that direction.

"Ooohh," Barb screamed and ran toward the men. "Steve! Steve!" The men stopped. One of them turned, and then he dropped his bag and ran toward them. Barb looked back and saw Eddie limping along as fast as he could move.

Of course, she reached her oldest brother first. Steve hugged her and swung her off her feet. Then he put her down and rushed toward Eddie and gave him the same treatment.

"We didn't know you were coming," Barb said. "Why didn't you call us?"

"I thought I'd surprise the family." He introduced his friends, who had a few hours to spend before catching the train for their homes, one in Montana, and the other in Idaho.

"Mama will be so surprised," Barb said.

When they got home, no one was there. Barb read Mama's note on the refrigerator.

"She won't be home until five. She and Isabel went downtown." Since war production was over, Isabel had been looking for a different job. Boeing didn't need so many workers. Dad still worked there, but now he had Sundays off and only worked eight hours a day.

Frank and Audrey came in from school, and the reunion continued. Alice walked in from the neighbor's and hugged Steve. She told him all about Jim, who had called several times from a hospital in California.

While they waited, Steve and the other soldiers lounged in the living room and entertained them with tales about the lighter side of life in the army. Steve moved over to the couch beside Barb.

"Every morning and every night, I read your bookmark," he told her. "It carried me through the bad parts of the war." He pulled the bookmark from his wallet. It was well worn and creased, but Barb's carefully printed words from the Twenty-third Psalm were still legible.

"God was with me," Steve said. "I constantly reminded myself of that and of the little girl who wanted to see me in one piece after the war." He tickled her sides. "You have sure grown up in the last few years."

Barb grinned. She was the shortest in her family, but at that moment she felt six feet tall.

"The home front kept us going," one of the soldiers said. "The Germans were running out of planes and bullets, but our supplies kept on coming."

"We sold war stamps at school," Eddie said. "And we raised a Victory garden."

"All your efforts brought us home," Steve said. He looked up at the commotion at the door as Mama and Isabel carried packages inside. "Hi, Mama," Steve said as conversationally as if he'd seen her just that morning.

For an instant, Mama froze. "Oh, Steve!" she wailed, and it was almost a repetition of the day that Alice found out that Jim was alive. She was still wiping tears of joy when Dad came home.

He shook Steve's hand and then pulled him close in a bear hug. "Son, we're so glad you're home."

Barb called Carolyn and told her. Carolyn seemed happy, but there was a moment when Barb's happiness was erased. While Carolyn didn't say anything, her tone of voice reminded Barb that Carolyn's brother wouldn't be coming home.

Steve's friends left that night, and Steve said he was going to do nothing for a week except sit on the front porch and look at the world from a peaceful view. Eddie tried to get him to talk about D-Day, but Steve said he couldn't talk about that yet. He wanted to look ahead, not backward.

Only a few days had passed before Steve was applying for temporary work until time for the January semester to start at the university, where he could attend on the GI Bill.

"If Uncle Sam wants to pay for my education," Steve said, "I guess I'll take him up on it."

A few days later, Yoko received a letter from her father. "He believes he will not be home for some time," she told Barb on the telephone. "But he has received many medals for his bravery. I am honored to be his daughter."

Fall days passed, and October turned to November. With no battle news to report, the newspapers and radio focused on the war crimes trials in Nuremberg, Germany. Barb was stunned by the charges against the Nazi leaders.

"I'm not going to read the paper ever again," she said after reading about the horrible things they had done. It made her feel that same awful pain in her stomach she'd felt when she saw the concentration camps on the newsreel.

"No need to bury your head in the sand," Steve said. "We must learn from this so it can never happen again. That's what we fought for."

Dad agreed. "It's fitting that a court settle up the end of the war. That's a civilized way to deal with a disagreement."

Two days before Thanksgiving the Nuremberg Trials began, and the radio newscast was filled with nothing else. But at Barb's house, the trials took a backseat to Jim Watson's arrival.

Alice had gone with the Watsons to meet Jim's train, and then they stopped by the house before taking him home.

He was not like Barb remembered. A very thin man came to the door with his arm possessively around Alice's shoulder as if he would never let her go. They sat beside each other on the couch. Alice smiled and kept her gaze on him even when his parents or someone else spoke.

"He may look a little different, but he's the same man who left here," she said. "I can see it in his eyes."

He lifted Alice's hand to his lips and kissed it. "You're more beautiful than ever," he said very softly, but Barb, who was sitting on his other side, heard it plainly.

"Tell us about the Bataan Death March," Eddie said.

A cloud passed over Jim's face. "I'd rather we talked about the future than the past right now."

"Okay," Eddie said quickly, and the others respected Jim's wishes, just as they had Steve's. Talk turned to Thanksgiving, and the Watsons agreed to come to dinner.

For two days, Barb and the girls cleaned and helped Mama cook. On Thursday morning the family rearranged the Harrington living room.

By moving furniture to the edges of the room and putting tables together, Steve and Frank created one long table. The girls set up the wooden folding chairs they'd borrowed from their church. Mama draped several cloths over the tables, and Barb and Eddie made place mats out of brown construction paper with horns of plenty on one side. On the other side, they wrote a name, so everyone would know where to sit.

After the Watsons and Jim, Aunt Daisy and Raymond, and the Wakamutsus and Yoko arrived, Mama and the girls carried the turkey and all the trimmings to the living room.

"Shall we have grace?" Dad asked. They all took their seats and joined hands. "Father, thank You for another Thanksgiving and this special one when we have so much to be thankful for. We are proud to be Americans and thank You for the freedoms we enjoy. Thank You for keeping our loved ones safe as they faced battle and for bringing them home to us. Amen."

"Amen" echoed around the table.

Barb looked around at her reunited family and added quietly, "God bless America."

Congratulations!

You have completed the American Adventure! We hope you've enjoyed your journey through more than 300 years of American history—from the sailing of the *Mayflower* to the conclusion of World War II.

You've traveled to places like colonial Boston and nineteenth-century Minneapolis, met important people like Theodore Roosevelt and Thomas Edison, and seen how God works in human lives. Now that you've discovered so many interesting events and fascinating people from our nation's history, perhaps you'll want to learn more on your own.

Your local library or bookstore will have lots of books on the people and time periods you enjoyed most in the American Adventure. Ask your parent or teacher for help in deciding which book is best. History is fun—so keep reading!!

You're in for the ultimate
American Adventure!
Collect all 48 books!